THE PHANTOM'S PHANTOM

A Novel of *The Phantom Detective Agency*

As Taken from the Case Files of
Richard Curtis Van Loan, The Phantom

For John Whisks, whose Imprimatur as Emperor of the Inland Empire made it all possible!

R [signature]

5-3-07

by

ROBERT REGINALD

Wildside Press, LLC
Rockville, Maryland
MMVII

CONTENTS

For

Tim Underwood

and

Geoff Smith

Two of My Phavorite Phantomimists

PROLOGUE

ENTER THE PHANTOM
▲
Old age is the most unexpected of all the things that happen to a man.
—Leon Trotsky
▼
SAN BERNARDINO, CALIFORNIA
20 NOVEMBER 2005

"Professor Simmons?"

I lifted my head with a sigh. I'd been dozing over the proofs of my latest article, "Some Anomalies in the Use of Celator Monograms in the Late Tetradrachms of King Dēmētrios III," for *The Journal of Selective Seleukid Studies*, and my scintillating prose had once again sent me off to Slumberland.

I glanced back at the door to my small office. A man stood there framed in the light. I couldn't make out his features, but I did observe a black coat and tie—unusual garb, to say the least, for the heat of an early California autumn.

"I'm sorry," I said, "but I don't recall your name. Which class are you in?"

"I am not with the university, sir," the "suit" replied.

He stepped forward and handed me his card.

"Jaye Jackson Polke," I read, "Attorney at Law, Polke, Polke, and Prödert," underlined with a prominent Park Avenue address in New York City.

I motioned him to the spare chair.

"So, Mr. Polke," I stated, "what can I do for you?"

"I am very sorry indeed, sir, to inform you that your uncle has passed on," he noted.

"Uncle? What uncle?" I asked.

"Percy Robert Wallis Simmons," Polke indicated. "He died several weeks ago at the age of one hundred and six years. You appear to be his only heir."

I thought for a moment.

"You mean Great-Uncle 'Liz'?" I replied. "But I remember reading his obit decades ago."

"Mr. Simmons did enjoy his practical jokes, sir," came the reply. "Nonetheless, the facts are precisely as I have stated."

"But, but...," I struggled to find some response. "I never even met the man, never knew him at all, never had any contact with him. And, and there are plenty of other heirs. I mean, Great-Aunt Honeysuckle Rose had ten children, and cousin Hack L. Berry had seven sons, and my uncle Horatio Horne, well, he...."

"You are designated as Mr. Simmons's sole beneficiary under the terms of his last will and testament."

Polke handed me a folder with the relevant documents.

I paged through the sheets. Sure enough, there was my moniker, Prof. Robert Reginald Burgess Simmons, highlighted every other paragraph or so.

"So what do I have to do?" I inquired.

"Mr. Simmons left very specific instructions. You will need to take possession of his Long Island estate no later than three months from this date in order to qualify."

"What!" I exclaimed. "But we're right in the middle of fall term. I just can't pick up and leave."

The lawyer shook his head and tsk-tsked at me.

"Sir, if you fail physically to enter the Edgewater estate within ninety days of this meeting, you will forever forfeit any right to Mr. Simmons's real and personal property."

"Uh, just how much are we talking about?" I asked.

Polke handed me another voluminous document.

I tried to make some sense of the numbers as I flipped through the sheets.

"What's the bottom line?" I inquired.

"The summary is on the final page," the attorney stated.

I flipped over the stack and read: "$241,687,033.92."

"This can't be right," I said.

"I assure you, sir, it is. Indeed, the figure is a very conservative one: there might be a few dollars more. The alternate beneficiary, should you fail to appear at Edgewater Estate within the time period specified by this document, is the Ferret Philanthropic Society of Philadelphia. Mr. Simmons did tend to dote on his little furry friends."

I assured Polke that the friendly ferrety folk would have to fend for themselves this year, and signed the agreement that he presented to me. We arranged an appointment at Edgewater during my academic break in early December.

* * * * * * *

6

My great-uncle's estate was not what I expected. Five buildings were scattered about the property, none of them well maintained. They included a tattered farmhouse, a guest facility, and several storage units. The furniture was old and well-worn, the fixtures long outdated.

"He didn't spend much on himself, did he?" I mused.

"Mr. Simmons was a parsimonious man, particularly in his later years," Polke commented.

He was acting as my guide for the day.

"Did you know him well?"

"I do not think that anyone knew Mr. Simmons well," came the response. "He was a private individual who kept to himself."

It was when we reached the third building that I made the discovery. This structure had the appearance of being an old guest house or servants' quarters, but had been remodeled at some point to eliminate the windows.

"What was this used for?" I queried.

"I really have no idea, sir," Polke replied. "I was never granted access to this particular place."

He opened the only door, a heavy steel barrier, with a special set of three keys. The entranceway sported several deadbolts. Pulling open the heavy structure with an "oomph," the attorney motioned me inside.

"I am not allowed to enter," he explained.

The lights came on automatically, and the door swung shut behind me without any assistance. I could hear a circulation system begin working in the background. There were three rooms inside.

The front area had obviously been Simmons's personal office, complete with desk, computer, the latest in communication devices, and, incongruously, an old Underwood typewriter.

A small restroom was located off to one side.

The third room provided the real revelation.

The walls were lined with books, row after row of them, including thousands of scholarly and popular works on crime and criminals, mystery novels from around the world, and a bank of what appeared to be leather-bound manuscripts.

I picked one up at random. "*Fangs of Murder*" the title blared. It was an old pulp story featuring someone called The Phantom Detective. Another volume was titled *Tycoon of Crime*. They were all part of the same series, filled with lurid prose, over-the-top villains, and a heroic crime-fighter righting wrongs and solving mysteries.

Pretty rum stuff overall, I thought.

I reshelved the books and examined the room again. A small desk rested to one side, and on it was an envelope addressed in a shaky hand to "Robert." I picked it up, slit the edge, and read the note inside.

7

"My Dear Nephew,

"When you see this, I will finally be gone. I regret not having contacted you when I could have done so, but I have never been the most social of men, and every time that I reached for the phone, I finally hesitated.

"I have, however, followed your career with some great interest, even lending a hand here and there where I thought that it might do you some good. I apologize for my occasional interference in your life, but I have never hesitated in the past to intervene when I thought I could make a positive difference in the outcome.

"You may have already guessed from the contents of my little hideaway that I, like you, was a writer of sorts, penning my lurid accounts of the Phantom under a *nom de plume* generated from my middle names. I never pretended to have any literary ability as such. My sole purpose was to record the exploits of my dear friend Richard, so that his pseudonymous memory might be preserved for yet another generation.

"He and I were very close. None of the stories recorded in my accounts were accurate as to specifics, but all reflected the reality of life in New York during the Depression and War years, when gangsters threatened to subvert the very fabric of American society. The man I call Richard Curtis Van Loan was one of the few individuals boldly to stand against evil during this time.

"I will not tell you his real name. Let him remain anonymous, as I insist upon maintaining my anomalous status as a writer. There were exploits of his that I could not publish at the time, for fear of having the details reveal too much about his—or my—identity. Neither of us ever wanted to be a public figure. There were also stories that occurred somewhat later in his career, after he had abandoned the mask and used his inheritance to assemble a crime-fighting team appropriate to the 1950s.

"I wrote them down anyway, and they are all here in this room. Publish them or not, as you will. 'Richard' never ceased fighting against the forces of evil. He was a great man and a good one. Follow in our footsteps, my dear boy, and do what you can to make a difference in the world. The choice is always yours.

"Your Uncle Percy."

I sat down in the only chair in the room, a hard upright of slatted wood, my wind knocked out of me by my uncle's unexpected missive.

I heard a distant pounding.

"Are you all right?" came a faint voice.

I hurried into the other room, opened the door, and carefully closed and locked the entrance behind me.

"Yes, I'm fine," I noted. "I'll be staying somewhat longer than I originally anticipated."

"Very good, sir," Polke stated. "You will need to sign this document to complete the transfer of Mr. Simmons's property, and then I am finished with this phase. We will make whatever financial arrangements you designate."

"Thank you, Polke," I replied, dismissing the man.

One thing about lawyers: when you need one, you need one, but otherwise they are completely and eminently disposable.

I retired from the university later that week.

It took me a month to take inventory of the contents of the Third Room, as I was now calling it, and to discover the shelf of unpublished (but neatly bound) manuscripts left to me by my uncle. They were written very much in his old style, with minimal characterization, lurid prose, and staccato-like action. I decided to spiff them up a bit before releasing them upon an unsuspecting world.

Finally, I decided upon the first new adventure of The Phantom Detective, the account that my uncle called *The Phantom's Phantom*. This particular episode was set in the immediate aftermath of the detective's initial retirement during the early 1950s, and was very different in tone and setting—indeed, in storyline—from any of the previous narratives.

But I found the crafting of the novel a bit tougher than I'd anticipated. This wasn't like my stuffy literary fictions that had graced the pages of such serious reviews as *Biquarterly*, *Shenandoah Showplace*, and *Tricuspid*.

I decided that I had to find a way of bringing out the man behind the mask, so to speak, even if the mask had been permanently retired.

So I reworked the narrative from the third person to the first, feeling that this reflected the inner voice of the detective in somewhat more vital and immediate detail. I also scaled back some of the verbiage of the original and focused instead on the characters.

This was the most personal of the Phantom stories that I discovered, and it was a good starting point, since it marked a significant change in Van Loan's approach to fighting crime—and to his life.

I think the events of the tale speak for themselves.

Finally, like my uncle, I used a reworked version of my real name as the byline on the new book.

This is the result.
This is The Phantom Detective as he appeared in later life.
This is *The Phantom's Phantom*.

I.

"I KNOW WHO YOU ARE!"

▲

You can't make an omelet without breaking some eggs.
—Old French Proverb

▼

New York, New York
Tuesday, 20 October 1953

"Are you dining alone, *Monsieur* Van Loan?"

I glanced at the green-coated *maître d'* of "Le Gnome Gastrique." He was hovering over me like a rotund frog gingerly approaching a fly, about to snag his unwary prey with his slimy tongue. He carefully took my hat and coat and handed them off to an attendant, holding them at arm's length, as if they needed to be swabbed with antiseptic.

I grimaced at the man's overt obsequiousness, part of the price that I paid for being a public figure.

"Miss Underhill and *Comte* Bâtonrompe will be joining me shortly, Jacques," I replied.

"Very good, *monsieur*: we have your usual table ready," came the reply. "If *vous* will follow me...."

I wound my way through a maze of dim-witted dignitaries and hoity-toity hierophants, which between them could probably scrape together no more than half a brain, idly waving my hand at the high and mighty of the Big Apple. I preferred a spot apart from the hustle and bustle of the vocalizing VIPs, and so I parked myself at my usual hideaway, right next to a picture window overlooking the Empire State Building. It sparkled in the distance like a giant roman candle, all aglitter with gloss and glitz and glamour.

The "Gnome" was located on the tenth—the top—floor of the Perry van Winkle Building in Manhattan. It specialized in *haute* French cuisine offered at exorbitant prices by swaggering sycophants swathed in slime-green attire, but I usually found that the fare justified the fracas. They had a master chef, M. Sirice Sétif, imported directly from Casablanca, who could twist a tasty tart as neatly as a Bowery pimp.

I caught a glimpse of myself reflected back from the glass. The figure in the makeshift mirror was slim and tall and slightly graying at

11

the temples. He might have been a broker or a banker, save for the carefully trimmed salt-and-pepper mustache brushing his upper lip, and the devil-may-care sparkle of his azure eyes. I tilted my head to one side, frowning at the lines creeping across the portrait, and was still musing on *la scène dramatique* when a woman's sultry voice cut right through my pretentiousness.

"Admiring yourself, Mr. Van Loan?"

I saw the svelte figure of Dastrie Lee Underhill sliding towards me through the *ménagerie*. She was the daughter of former Police Commissioner T. Edward "Fast Eddie" Underhill, who was known not so much for his crime-fighting qualities as his ability to generate additional revenue streams for his department. He'd survived and prospered under Mayors LaGuardia and O'Dwyer until he'd finally stumbled over a scandal that even he couldn't hide. His young daughter had come to me then and begged for my assistance, and I'd done what I could to salvage the family's honor and reputation.

Dastrie was a sight well worth waiting for, with a lime-yellow Gibecière/Haillon-Neux gown draped off one alabaster shoulder, and a small gold Arcaneau handbag dangling heavily from her left wrist. Her figure filled all the right niches in all the right places, and her fine auburn hair swept down her neck in a waterfall of waves that captivated away her many admirers. She might have been twenty-five or thirty, but something in her wry expression and the crooked smile touching her ruby-red lips proclaimed an experience much broader, much crueler than her years.

I rose to my feet and extended my hand in greeting.

"My dear," I said, and then noticed the short, stubby man in the penguin-like tuxedo trailing along behind her.

"*Le Comte* Bâtonrompe," I added, bowing my head.

"It's been just *ages*, Richard!" Dastrie exclaimed.

"I've been away on business," I responded.

"Back to *La Cochinchine*?" the count inquired.

Bâtonrompe was a fat little man of some sixty years, with a small gray goatee plastered on his chin and a balding pate, the remaining strands of gray hair draping off the sides of his head like off-colored icicles. He'd represented the French Résistance during the late war, raising funds in North America and secretly funneling the arms and matériel he purchased to the freedom fighters abroad. He and I had collaborated on several ventures over the years.

"No," I stated. "Just, uh, doing a favor for a friend."

"A terrible thing zeez eez, *la guerre annamite*," Bâtonrompe rambled on, not really speaking to anyone in particular. "We win zee battle, *Monsieur* Van Loan, but zee war, she just goes on and on."

"Indeed," I agreed, not really wanting to go down this road.

The French government had grabbed a scorpion by its tail in Indochina, and would soon feel the terrible thrust of its sting. And that was the best outcome possible; there were many potential bad ones.

"It's so good to have you back again," Dastrie exhaled. "*Monsieur le Comte* was telling me how much he appreciates your company. He enjoys watching the ladies chase you 'round and 'round the marriage bed, without ever reeling you in."

"I guess I'm just a confirmed bachelor," I acknowledged, not wanting to venture down *that* particular pathway either!

"*Je suis* Poupongris," a voice interrupted, "zee one who will have zee honor of serving *vous*! Are *vous* ready to order, *mademoiselle et monsieurs*?"

The waiter was new to the place. I'd never seen him before.

"*Oui!*" Count Bâtonrompe replied. "If you do not mind, *mes amis*"—He glanced around the table at us, and we both nodded our agreement—"we begin with zee oyster-cloisters and zee '33 Château des Hommes-Grenouilles, if zeez will meet with your approval.

"Zen, we continue with *le bœuf en conserve avec hachis, les cuisses de grenouille en une pâtisserie des escargots, le canard sauvage à la myrtille*, and yes, finally, as zee *pièce de résistance, le flan des œfs à la coque.*"

"Quite, quite unique, *monsieur*," I commented, shaking my head at this *fait accompli de la cuisine*.

He bobbed his head up and down, almost giggling in his enthusiasm. One thing about the count: he always enjoyed his meals.

"What's all that gibberish about, Richard?" Dastrie asked. "I didn't understand any of it."

"Just a few odds and ends, my dear," I stated, smiling at her. "Now, whatever have you been doing during my absence?"

There followed a long rendition of miscellaneous social encounters and parties and elite functions, none of which interested me in the slightest. I maintained a polite demeanor while each delicious course was served, one after the other.

We were starting on the culminating custard when the *maître d'* returned.

"A call for you, *Monsieur* Van Loan," he announced. "You can take it up front."

"Excuse me, please," I said, and then I followed Jacques (whose real name, I knew, was Jack Strunsky of The Bronx) to the telephone station set aside for the guests.

"Van?" came a faint female voice on the other end of the line. "Van? They told me you were dining there."

"Cyndi?"

"He's dead, Van! Frank's dead!"

13

I sat down hard on the stool in the alcove, stunned by the news. Frank Havens was my oldest friend, one of just three persons who knew the real identity of The Phantom Detective. Indeed, he'd been the individual primarily responsible for putting me on the road to fighting crime, when I was at loose ends after the first war, despairing over ever finding a purpose to my life again after all the horrors of that conflict.

Frank had retired, sold off his publishing empire, and then moved to California, buying a small weekly there. I took it as a sign that it was time for The Phantom to retire as well. I was unwilling to risk my life in establishing a new contact to bridge the chasm between the police and the underworld. Indeed, the last of my old adventures had just recently been published by my official chronicler, the fictitious "Robert Wallace," and I was determined that there'd be no more, ever again.

Cynthia Havens was Frank's second and much younger wife. I'd known Mildred Havens very well, but had never been particularly close to Cyndi or her two young children. It was Mildred's daughter Muriel whom I'd nearly married once.

"They claim he committed suicide," Cyndi was saying, "but I don't believe it. He told me to contact you if anything queer ever happened to him. I think he was almost expecting this. You've got to help, Van. No one here will investigate his death!"

"Of course I will," I replied. "I'll cancel all my appointments and fly out tomorrow. And I'm truly sorry, Cyndi: Frank was a great and good man. How's Muriel taking it?"

"She's crushed, of course, just like all the rest of us. It's just awful, Van, every bit of it. What am I going to do? Please come as soon as possible."

"I'm already on my way."

After she hung up, I dialed another number.

"Lizzie," I ordered my secretary, "please book me a flight to Los Angeles tomorrow morning, quickest way possible. I'll also need a car and driver at the other end, nothing fancy, mind, and preferably someone who knows his way around the Redlands and San Bernardino area."

"Something wrong?" she asked.

"Frank Havens has died," I replied. "The circumstances are unusual, and I may have to stay out there awhile. Don't worry about the return ticket."

"Sure thing, boss," Lizzie replied. "I'll have your itinerary tonight. I'll also ask Roscoe to pack your bags."

Roscoe was my manservant, and I don't know what I'd do without either of them.

When I returned to our table, Dastrie noticed the expression on my face, and immediately expressed concern.

"My old friend Frank Havens is dead," I murmured.

"That's terrible!" she responded, but before she could say anything further, our waiter suddenly reappeared, clad in the standard emerald stripes sported by the restaurant staff.

"Jacques, he asked me to give you this, *monsieur!*" the man exclaimed, holding out a white card in his left hand.

As I leaned forward to take the square of stiff paper, the attendant suddenly whipped his right hand from behind his back, revealing a black, stub-nosed, .38-caliber revolver. Then he calmly, coldly, and methodically put six shots into the chest of Count Bâtonrompe. The body of the diplomat slumped over on top of me, the man's ruby red fluids gushing forth from his wounds. I tried to extricate myself, but the inert mass of the nobleman prevented me from moving. The shooter could easily have killed me then and there, if that had been his intent. My head was still reeling from the loud bangs and the mixed odor of blood and gunpowder and the sheer horror of it all.

But Dastrie just reached into her chic little handbag, pulled out a pearl-handled .22 pistol, quietly and quickly took aim, and plugged the murderer twice in the middle of his forehead. Only a few seconds had passed. The man teetered a moment, and then fell backwards into a platter of crab-and-shrimp *pâté* arrayed artistically on the adjoining table. The lady sitting there just looked down at the double-pierced skull of the assailant grinning up at her from her plate and started screaming her bloody lungs out. She wouldn't stop yelling until someone finally hauled her away.

I grunted hard as I pushed and prodded and propped the heavy body of the fat Frenchman upright in his chair, and then glanced over at the smoking end of my companion's potent weapon.

"My," I said, "we're just full of surprises tonight, aren't we, my dear?"

Dastrie smiled sweetly back at me, her white-tipped incisors glinting gaily in the candlelight.

"We all have our little secrets, Richard," she replied.

Then I realized that I was still clutching the three-by-five-inch card in my right hand. I glanced down at it.

On one side, printed very neatly in embossed Times Roman serifs, was emblazoned the supposed identity of the sender or receiver:

"THE PHANTOM'S PHANTOM."

On the reverse, a message had been hand-lettered in all caps.

"I KNOW WHO YOU ARE!" it proclaimed.

But who are you? I wondered silently.

I glanced around the restaurant. From each table I spied diners staring back at me, horror etched on their faces, hands covering their mouths. This was not the exquisite, exclusive experience that each had been expecting this evening.

15

"What does it say?" Dastrie asked.

"It says that a truly bad day just got a little worse," I stated.

I slipped the message into my inside coat pocket and asked for the check. I didn't think I'd be adding a tip!

Then Dastrie and the Count and I just waited for the police to arrive. I knew we'd have some hard questions to answer—and one of us wouldn't be saying a thing.

It was going to be a very long evening.

II.

"I KNOW WHAT YOU DO!"
▲

As many arrows, loosèd several ways, fly to one mark.
——William Shakespeare
▼

ON ROUTE FROM NEW YORK TO LOS ANGELES
WEDNESDAY, 21 OCTOBER 1953

And, in fact, the police kept us for questioning about the "wee incident" until the "wee" hours of the following morning, but I could tell them nothing more than I'd seen: the assassination itself and Dastrie's response to it. For some reason, they seemed significantly less interested in the latter than they should have been, which told me rather more, I suspect, than they wanted me to know. Count Boèce du Bâtonrompe had been attached to the French delegation at the UN, and I wondered how Miss Underhill had burrowed her way under the nobleman's defenses.

My contacts with the NYPD had sadly and rapidly diminished after the war, particularly following the retirement of Capt. Gregg, my old adversary; there was no one left any longer on whom I could call to end this interminable farce, other than one old sergeant out in the precincts. Finally the boys in blue just gave up and let me go "home," although by that time of the morning, home in this case was just too far away to reach and still be able to make my morning flight. I settled instead for my suite in the Brockleigh-Greeneleaffe Building, where I kept a cot handy for just this purpose.

Lizzie had arranged my departure from LaGuardia Airport at 9:21 that same day, the Twenty-First, so I rose promptly at six, exercised, showered in the closet-like bathroom adjoining my office, changed into a fresh suit, and quickly examined the travel bags that Roscoe had put together the previous evening. All was in order. I breakfasted down the block at Briskets 'n' Bagels, and was back again at 7:20, by which time Lizzie already had the day's business ready for me to review. I signed the several documents that absolutely couldn't wait until my return and set aside the others, giving her detailed instructions to cover my absence. By eight I was pell-melling out the door, hailing a Yellow Cab.

17

My ownership of a sizable block of TWA stock allowed me to enter the Lockheed L-1049 Super Constellation before anyone else, handing my two suitcases to an attendant. I then settled into a spacious first-class seat, already exhausted.

The SuperCons were roomy aircraft with a three-pronged tail and a hunched-over look that gave them the appearance of lying in wait to pounce on their unsuspecting victims. But their four oversized, powerful propellers and large fuel capacity allowed them to make the non-stop flight from coast to coast with relative ease in just nine hours, and that's all that mattered to me on this trip. I cracked open a copy of Ernest K. Gann's newest bestseller, *The High and the Mighty*, an ironically appropriate read for my journey.

Someone sat down in the seat next to me, but I paid her no mind. I was already engrossed in the author's tense story of a distressed DC-4 fighting for its survival over the Pacific Ocean. Indeed, I barely felt our own craft begin to move, although I did look up briefly when it paused at the head of the runway to rev up its engines, testing each one sequentially before committing itself to the final leap into space.

About an hour into the flight my too-short night finally caught up with me, and I fell asleep holding the book open on my lap. I vaguely felt someone lift it from my outstretched hands.

"Excuse me, sir," the stewardess was saying to me, leaning over the pretty woman to my left (whom I now noticed for the first time). "Do you want lunch?"

"Uh, yes please," I replied, sitting up and stretching: "A salad, if you will, some ice water, and a piece of fruit—an apple if you have it."

"Of course, sir. What kind of dressing?"

"Vinegar and oil on the side, please, or just vinaigrette—and pepper, lots of pepper. Thanks."

I caught a glimpse of a hastily squashed smile on the face of my traveling companion.

"Hope I didn't disturb you with my snoring," I said.

"You *were* rather out of it for a while," she responded. "But I saved your place for you," handing the novel back to me.

She was about thirty years of age, dark-haired, brown-eyed, petite, and well-dressed, with the small accouterments of jewelry and clothing and style that shouted "MONEY" to anyone who'd pay attention—and she definitely wanted all the attention that she could get.

"Business or pleasure?" she asked.

"I'm sorry," I said, "what?"

I still wasn't completely alert, and for a moment I thought she'd meant something entirely different.

"Oh," I finally replied. "An old friend died. I'm going out to his funeral."

"I'm dreadfully sorry."

She was quiet for a moment.

"I'm Gabrielle Guest, by the way."

"Richard Van Loan."

We shook hands.

"Are you a businessman, Mr. Van Loan?"

"Retired," I said. "And you?"

She laughed out loud, a small tinkling sound like the distant chant of wind chimes chirping on a sleepy summer afternoon.

"An aspiring actress," she said. "It's a business of a sort, I guess, when it works."

"And does it work for you?" I asked.

"Not all the time. I'm supposed to be auditioning for a new role."

"You *seem* to be doing well by all appearances."

"My *ex-husband* is doing very well, Mr. Van Loan," she stated, "which means I do well also. But as an actress, I'm still struggling, I'm afraid."

Then lunch arrived.

Afterwards I fell asleep again. I just couldn't help myself.

The lurch of the aircraft woke me a few hours later.

"Thunderstorm," Gabrielle said, nodding towards the window.

I glanced outside: threatening black clouds were swirling all around us

Again the plane moved violently up and then down, up and down.

"Oh, God, I'm going to be sick," my seatmate exclaimed.

She hastily reached into the pocket ahead of her, pulled out a paper bag, and exhaled her lunch. She had to vomit several more times before we passed out of the turbulence.

"I'm so, *so* sorry," she apologized. "I just don't know what got into me. Excuse me, please," she added, heading towards the restroom.

She had more color in her delicious cheeks (good enough to eat!) when she returned a few moments later, obviously much refreshed. She asked the stewardess for some seltzer water.

By supper Gabrielle had regained her appetite sufficiently to order the fish filet. I had the steak, which I found barely passable: the potatoes were undercooked, the vegetables overcooked, the bread singed black, and the meat, well, the meat was second-string at best and stringy at worst. Still, I was sufficiently hungry to consume half of the mess before finally giving it up.

Over the Mojave Desert we again encountered some turbulence, and my companion was violently ill once more.

"Ohhh," she exclaimed, "I just want to curl up and die somewhere."

"You'll feel better once we're back on solid ground," I noted. "Really!"

"I think I'll try the powder-room again," she indicated, toddling off to the facilities.

She was gone much longer this time, and when she returned, her face was still a pasty white.

"I don't feel so good," she stated.

I flagged down the stewardess and ordered a bicarbonate of soda.

"Thank you so much," she said, when the bubbly finally arrived. She sipped a few swallows. "Oh, I almost forgot, Mr. Van Loan. I found this sitting on the basin in the restroom."

She handed me another of the small white cards.

"It was addressed to you. Isn't that so strange?"

"Very," I replied.

The obverse was exactly the same as the previous note.

I turned it over.

"VAN LOAN: I KNOW WHAT YOU DO!" it read.

"What does it mean?" she asked.

Then she burped and groaned very loudly.

"Oh my," Gabrielle gasped. "It really hurts."

"Where?" I asked, now greatly concerned.

"Right down in my belly," she said. "Ohhh!"

A stewardess suddenly appeared.

"What's the matter?" she wanted to know.

"We need a doctor here," I stated.

But there was none on board save a balding veterinarian from Portland named Dr. Marquis, and he could do nothing for Miss Guest. By the time we reached Los Angeles International Airport, she was dead, a milky froth dripping from her lips. It looked suspiciously like some sort of alkaloid poisoning.

The police in Los Angeles obviously shared similar thoughts. They sequestered all of the passengers until we could be questioned, over and over and over again. Of course, they particularly focused their attention on me, since I'd occupied the adjoining seat.

"I don't know anything," I told them, but I didn't mention the card: that was *my* business.

I explained to them my sole reason for traveling to California, that I'd never before met the deceased—which was true—and that I had no idea of what had happened to her—a possible prevarication. They finally released me at four in the morning West Coast Time (three hours earlier than Eastern Time!). Somehow I secured a room at the Hotel Börschbietz, where I finally tumbled into the welcoming white shrouds of a lovely, lovely bed, and slept away the dying hours of the morning in the sleep of the utterly righteous—or the sighs of the grateful dead.

III.

"I KNOW WHERE YOU GO!"

▲

There is a shadow under this red rock.
—T. S. Eliot

▼

REDLANDS, CALIFORNIA
THURSDAY, 22 OCTOBER 1953

I left a wakeup call for eight and ordered my car for ten; but even so, was barely able to finish my *tai chi chuan* routine, shower, shave, dress, pack, munch a light breakfast, and still "get me to the church on time," as the old song says. I settled my bill and rushed outside, but, of course, no one was there.

I took advantage of the unaccustomed break to ponder the events of the last few days. Someone was stalking me—but why? When I'd retired two years earlier, it had seemed the appropriate thing to do at the time. Frank Havens had been my last connection with New York officialdom, and he was departing for points west. Muriel, Frank's daughter, had long since married a physician and then relocated to California to raise her two children, although I'd never understood why, since she was very close to her father. My ties to the metropolitan police had quickly withered away after Gregg's retirement in 1950.

As for me, well, in these latter days of the "Communist threat" and big-power brinksmanship, I was in danger of becoming an object of ridicule if I continued playing the same old game. Somehow, sporting a mask while trying to hold back the ever-diminishing forces of evil no longer seemed *de rigueur*. Most folks were focused on the threat from Eastern Europe.

And why now? Who'd managed to uncover the closely guarded secret of my former identity? Who even cared these days?

I thought about my options. With Frank gone, there really wasn't anyone else on whom I could call for assistance. The NYPD, if they learned my true identity, might well arrest me for having worked outside the law once too often. The FBI wouldn't *dare* touch me—I had too much dirt stashed away about their fascist, cross-dressing leader—but neither would they lift an administrative finger to help. They'd just laugh

21

in my face. The local authorities in California were unknown to me, and I to them. This was Terra Incognita I was entering. The problem was, I now had no official credentials and no legal identity as a crime-fighter. I didn't even qualify for a private dick's license there.

But that wasn't the only thing. My energy just wasn't the same any longer. Oh, I still kept fit and still had my brains, to be sure; but I knew that this wasn't enough to handle a situation like this, where I was a fish out of water. California was a very different place indeed from what I was used to. I needed to find some way of defending myself from this unknown adversary—and fast!

"*Señor* Van Loan?"

I looked up at a short Hispanic man in his mid-twenties holding open the back door of a Ford wagon. I'd deliberately requested a vehicle that would melt into the background of any social or economic environment. It wasn't stylish, but it'd do quite handily, thank you.

"*¿Cómo se llama usted?*" I asked the driver.

"*Me llamo* Tigrán el Grande Aguilera del Fausto y Durán, at your service, *señor*," the driver replied. "But you, you can call me Tigre."

The little man actually bowed to me, doffing his beaked cap.

"Tigrán el Grande, eh," I mused, "the ancient Armenian king."

"*¡Sí, señor!* Me and *mi hermanos*, we were naméd after the great *reyes* of the olden days: Alejandro el Grande, Julio-César, Constantino el Grande, Antíoco Primero, Salomón el Rey,..."

"I understand," I interjected, afraid that the recitation might go on for days. "Do you know Redlands and San Bernardino?"

"*Sí, señor. Mi padre*, he works there for *El Ferrocarril de Santa Fé*, what you call the 'rayel-road.' Me, I can find you the Red-Lands or San Bernardino or El Coltón or any other place that you wish to go. I know all the *calles*. I do very good job for you, you see, *señor*."

He nodded his head vigorously up and down, his unruly mop of black hair flopping in time, and then he motioned towards the open door.

Soon we were heading south towards the broad fields of Orange County. The countryside here was filled with vegetable farms and fruit orchards, a vista very different from what I was used to back east. Before long, though, I found myself dozing in the comfortable rear seat. The change in time and the chronic lack of sleep were beginning to wear me down.

I woke when the Ford hit a pothole, and suddenly found myself ravenous again.

"Tigre, please stop whenever you see a place to eat," I ordered.

A few minutes later, we pulled into the dusty entrance of a deteriorating taco stand called "El Perro Gordo," which my driver pronounced with a great and gusty rolling of his "R"s. The faded image of a fat yellow dog sitting up and begging adorned the front flank of the establishment.

"You sure about this?" I asked.

The café looked pretty seedy to me.

"*Señor*, I know thees place," Tigre replied. "The *chiles rellenos* are best in all of California del Sur."

"Rellenos? What's that?"

"It ees the food of the gods, *señor!*"

They looked to me like nothing more than giant yellow slugs squatting on the paper plates amidst the beans and rice, but they smelled pretty damned good to my empty stomach, so I tried them anyway, washing them down with a bottle of cold brew marked with several "x"s on its side. I made the mistake, though, of stuffing a very large bite into my mouth, and when I finally caught my breath again, I was already chugging down my second beer to put out the fire inside. In the end, I finally had to agree that the fried green chiles filled with cheese and covered with tomato sauce were...*hot, hot, hot!*—but absolutely delicious nonetheless. I'd never eaten anything like them.

The locals thought that the huffings and puffings of the strange *gringo* were remarkably amusing, but I took their gibes in due course, and bought them all a round of Dos Equis, which they seemed to appreciate. They toasted *"El Gringo Viejo"* and *"El Brujo del Este"* and several other names as well.

There were many other things on the menu, if a handwritten list tacked on the wall could be called such, and I would have liked to have tried them all, but we had to be on our way. I paid the proprietor, Pepino Encurtido, two dollars—way too much, Tigre assured me afterwards: "You will let me deal with these *cholos* in the future, eh, *señor!*"

It took us three hours to reach Redlands, a small community in the so-called Inland Empire of Southern California. The mid-afternoon sun was blazing hot, even at this late date in the year.

We pulled into the parking lot of the local train station, where Muriel Rowlings and her spouse were waiting for us.

"Van!" she exclaimed, rushing forward to embrace me.

It had been years since I'd last seen her: she was becoming almost matronly.

She motioned to the man standing behind her.

"You've met Kenneth," she indicated. "He's a local GP."

"Good to see you again, sir," I responded, offering my hand.

He offered the firm, wet grasp of a leech.

"If you'll just trail us out of town," Muriel stated, "we'll take you right out to the ranch. We'll be heading down Highway 99 to Live Oak Canyon Road, and then following the creek southwest until we almost

23

reach the railroad tracks and San Timoteo Canyon. Twin Pines Rancho is located on the left just before the crossroads."

"I understand, *señora*," Tigre stated.

Before we went any further, though, I just had to remove my coat and tie. It must have been touching the mid-90s out there, and I was dying from the unexpected heat.

The rolling hills outside the town were brown and sere in the blazing autumn sun, but the setting had a certain stark beauty all its own. Stubby oaks dotted the landscape here and there, punctuated by the occasional house or ranch set back from the road, their perfectly aligned fences crowded with cattle and horses and even sheep on occasion.

"Beautiful countryside," I murmured to myself.

"*Sí, señor.* It ees like the old México I once knew in Oaxaca," my driver said.

We traveled twenty minutes over the straight highway and winding back road to reach Twin Pines, closely following the heels of Muriel's new Studebaker. The well-kept house and barn were set a few hundred feet back at the end of a long gravel driveway. Frank had planted several acres in barley and oats. I could also see a large garden sprouting just behind the main structure, and a well-kept corral and stable.

Cynthia Havens was waiting at the front door to greet us, her eyes red and face drawn, her thin body looking tired and worn, much older than her four decades, much older, in fact, than the last time I'd seen her. I ordered Tigre to park the car 'round the side and wait there for my instructions. Cyndi said he could help himself to refreshments in the kitchen. Then she turned to me.

"Thank you so much for coming, Van," she stated. "I just wish you could have visited us under better circumstances. Frank truly loved this place."

"He was a good man, the best I ever knew," I said. "You have my deepest sympathy, all of you."

I hugged her just once.

"You haven't seen our children in some time," she said. "This is Mellie"—a blonde girl in her early teens wandered out the door—"and Frankie"—a boy of about ten poked his face through the lace curtains of one window.

"And this is my daughter, Mitra," Muriel added, nodding at a pretty, black-haired girl of about nine. "Kenny's still in school."

The children were dispatched on various chores as the adults gathered together in the living room.

"Tell me what happened," I said to Cyndi.

"On Monday morning Frank drove to his office in Redlands as usual," she stated.

"*Where* in Redlands?" I asked.

"The newspaper's called *The Redlander*. The building's on the south side of Citrus near Sixth Street.

"About mid-morning, his secretary later told me, he received a phone call that upset him. He told Betty he had to meet someone for lunch and wasn't sure when he'd be back."

"Where did he go?"

"She didn't know. Redlands doesn't have much beyond the usual cafés and burger joints. It could have been anywhere. I mean, I always fixed him a sack lunch to take with him."

"Including Monday?"

"Yes. It was setting there on his desk, uh, afterwards."

"Then what happened?"

"He just never came home. He never went back to work either. About seven that evening I got a call from the San Bernardino County Sheriff's office saying that Frank's car had been hit by a train on San Bernardino Avenue near an orange grove northeast of town. They said the vehicle had stalled and Frank had tried to get out, but just staggered down the track in front of the train. The engineer couldn't stop in time."

"I went down to identify the body," Kenneth stated, picking up the narrative. "It was in pretty bad shape. They found a note in the car, but it didn't make much sense, according to the sheriff."

"Did you see the note yourself?"

"No."

"Anything else you can tell me?"

"Daddy seemed, well, out of sorts recently," Muriel commented. "I think something was troubling him, but he wouldn't tell me what it was."

"I felt the same thing," Cyndi agreed, "but when I asked him about it last week, he just said it was 'old business,' and that he had to take care of it himself. He was also having trouble sleeping this past month. And I found a receipt a few weeks ago: he'd withdrawn $500 in cash from our bank account. When I asked him about it, he just snapped at me, which was very unlike him, and wouldn't say what it was for. I almost think someone was blackmailing him."

"When's the funeral?"

"Saturday," several people said simultaneously.

"And none of you think it was suicide?"

"No!" they all chimed in.

"Frank would never kill himself, Van, not under any circumstance," Cyndi indicated. "He just wasn't that kind of man. He always faced his problems squarely. *We* always faced them together. I don't understand any of this."

"I'll try to see the sheriff tomorrow," I indicated. "You realize, though, that I can't conduct an official investigation in California. I don't have a license."

"We know that, Van," Muriel replied, "but anything you can do would help. Daddy always said to call you if anything happened to him. In fact, he reiterated it to me last month."

"I wonder why just now," I mused.

"Can you stay to dinner?" Cyndi asked.

"Thanks anyway," I responded, "but I'm really very tired from the trip. I need to get settled for the night. However, I'd like to visit Frank's office before then, if one of you could phone there and let them know that I'm coming, and that I have your authority to question anyone. That would help tremendously."

"Of course," Cyndi said.

Tigre and I reached Redlands again just before 4:30. Betty, Frank's secretary, was waiting for us at *The Redlander* office.

I introduced myself.

"Yes, sir," the secretary replied. "Mrs. Havens just phoned. I'm happy to help any way I can. I'm just sorry you couldn't have come sooner."

"Sooner? What do you mean?" I wanted to know.

"When Mr. Havens wrote you, sir."

"Recently?"

I was puzzled, since I hadn't had a note from Frank in months.

"Several weeks ago, Mr. Van Loan. I typed the letter myself."

"Do you have a copy?"

"I'm sure there's one in the files," Betty indicated.

"Before we look for that, I was told that Mr. Havens received an unsettling phone call on Monday," I stated.

"Yes, sir, his direct line rang, and then his voice rose in anger."

"Could you make out the words?"

"No, sir," Betty replied. "But he came out of his office immediately afterwards with hat in hand, said that he had some errands to run, and then was going to meet a friend for lunch. He seemed upset to me. He rushed out the door but returned almost immediately, saying he'd forgotten something. I glimpsed him through the open doorway taking a small object out of his top desk drawer. It might have been a passbook."

"For the bank?"

"Yes, sir."

"Did he often eat lunch outside the office?" I asked.

"Almost never. His wife fixed him a good meal each and every day. He said it helped keep his weight down."

"I'd like to examine his things now, if you don't mind."

"Of course, sir."

26

Betty led the way into the plainly furnished office, and unlocked the catches on the filing cabinet and the top right-hand desk drawer. She retrieved a file labeled "VAN LOAN" and pulled out the carbon copy of a letter. I read it carefully.

"Do you know what this says?" I asked.

"Yes, sir. As I said, I typed all of Mr. Havens's correspondence."

"I never received it."

"Well, I put it in the outgoing mail tray," she indicated, "but it was soon covered by the other letters, and I never actually saw the postman arrive that day."

I read it through a second time:

"Dear Van,

"The strangest thing has happened here, and I thought you ought to know. Perhaps a month ago I found a small white card in the middle of my desk. On one side it read, 'THE PHANTOM'S PHANTOM,' and on the other, 'I KNOW WHO YOU ARE.' I thought it was someone's idea of a joke, but no one in the office would admit to putting it there. I don't know who could have done it. My office is normally locked except when I'm here.

"This was the first of a series of such notes, each more ominous than the last. I'm enclosing them herewith. I think the target is obvious. Whoever wrote these lines intends to find and destroy what has been so carefully hidden. If something happens to me, I beg you to uncover the truth and to protect my dear wife and children and grandchildren. I know you'll do the right thing.

"I'm sorry to be such a burden to you, my friend, but I don't think the harassment will stop just because I want it to. I'm not afraid of dying, but I do fear for my family. Help me. Help them. Please.

"Frank"

"Did you see the cards he refers to?" I pressed.

"I saw some of them, sir," Betty stated, "but I didn't pay them much mind. This is a busy office and I have many other duties here. All of the cards were with the letter, except the final one, which arrived just last week."

"Do you know where that is?"

"I assume it's still here, sir," she indicated.

I dismissed her with the words, "Thank you, Miss Defoe," and then closed the door.

I took a moment to stand in the exact center of the room, and then slowly rotated in a 360-degree circle. I could see nothing out of the ordinary, but I wasn't that familiar with the original contents. Pictures of Frank's family lined the adjoining bookshelves.

I went through the filing cabinet first, but everything there seemed to be routine business correspondence. Then I searched the desk.

A small private drawer finally regurgitated something of interest. It was another of the three-by-five-inch cards, done in the same hand as all the others.

On the obverse it said: "THE PHANTOM'S PHANTOM."

On the reverse were the words, "I KNOW WHERE YOU GO!"

I also found a personal calendar in the same drawer. For Monday Frank had written, "Call RN." I paused for a moment. Who was "RN"? However, no actual appointments were listed for the final day of his life. Two weeks earlier, however, I found a 3:00 PM meeting scheduled with the same mysterious stranger.

"Miss Defoe," I stated, opening the door again, "do you know who this is?"

I showed her the entry.

"No, sir," she replied. "I know Mr. Havens went home early that day. He didn't tell me why."

"Did any of your staff resign in recent months?"

"No, can't think of a one."

"What about temporary help?"

"We haven't had any recently."

"Hmm." I was stumped. Then another possibility occurred to me: "Is anyone currently on vacation?"

"Yes, sir, one of our typesetters, John Nemo."

I laughed out loud.

"Of course," I said, mostly to myself. "Nemo means 'no one' in Latin. When was Mr. Nemo hired?"

"Uh, I think about six months ago. I could find out."

"Please do," I ordered. "Also, I'd like a copy of his employment record. You can send them both to me at the Hot Springs Hotel. What was Nemo like, Betty?"

"Well, sir, he was thin and plain and about average in height, and he had a slight mustache. He was maybe thirty years old."

"No photos, I assume."

"No, sir."

"Well, thanks so kindly for all your help and for staying past closing time to answer my questions. I think I'm through here," I indicated. "I'll take the calendar and card with me, if that's OK."

"Mrs. Havens said that you were to have access to everything, sir."

Tigre was waiting patiently outside. I ordered him to drive to the Hot Springs Hotel north of San Bernardino, and then gave him his release for the night.

He told me that he could stay with his parents on the west side of town, but I booked him into a separate room, wanting to have his services readily available to me.

At the front desk I signed the guest register of the posh resort, and then had an excellent T-bone steak in the Palmatoria Room, swished down with a '35 Château l'Antarctique. Scrumptious! I wanted to try the nearby hot springs to soak away some of my aches and cares, but needed to make a few phone calls first.

Friday was going to be another busy day.

IV.

"I KNOW WHERE YOU SLEEP!"
▲

Done ninety days in San Berdoo,
Can't find myself no one to sue.
—Boden Clarke
▼

SAN BERNARDINO, CALIFORNIA
FRIDAY, 23 OCTOBER 1953

The Hot Springs Hotel and Spa, sometimes called the Saetilla, had long been a weekend destination for the high and mighty of Los Angeles. The "old girl" had been destroyed three times over the decades by the periodic brush fires that plagued the San Bernardino Mountains, but on each occasion had been rebuilt even larger and grander than before, the last time in 1939. The history of the place was filled with the scandalous escapades of scantily clad Hollywood film starlets and rich muck-a-mucks from the global elite.

The ringing of a bell stirred me from a sound sleep.

"Yeah," I grumbled into the receiver.

"I KNOW WHERE YOU SLEEP!" a muffled voice hissed at me.

"What?" I responded, instantly awake.

But all I got in response was the distant click of a phone being reseated on its stand.

"Damn!" I exclaimed, swinging my legs down to the floor. "This has got to stop!"

I pulled out the phone directory and dived into the yellow pages. I tried dialing a number that I found there, but it was too early to get a response (I was still operating on East Coast time). I jotted it down on the notepad that the resort had so kindly provided me.

Then I ran through my morning routine of exercises, mental and physical, the fastidious cleansing of body and soul that I'd practiced now for some twenty years. After a shower and shave, I dressed and went down to a leisurely breakfast. I would, I decided, take things in order as they came.

I followed up on the messages that I'd sent the previous evening, and then made one additional call, redialing the number that I'd tried earlier, this time making a connection—and also an appointment. I now had my schedule set for the day. It was almost nine, the time when my driver was due to appear out front.

"The County Courthouse," I ordered Tigre as I entered the Ford.

"*Sí, señor.*"

The seat of the government of the County of San Bernardino, the largest county in the continental United States, was located in a massive, barn-like structure on Arrowhead Avenue. Everything was old about the place, from the brass-plated spittoons to the antique elevators, and I strongly suspected that County Supervisors' governance was equally as creaky.

Once I found my way through the maze of corridors, I was immediately ushered into the office of Sheriff William Jardine. He was a burly man of about fifty, with a rusty old six-shooter hanging off his right hip. If he'd ever actually tried firing that antique, the damn thing would've probably blown up in his face.

"I received a goddam unusual message this morning, Mr. Van Loan," the lawman indicated, motioning me to sit. "The Chairman of the Board of Supervisors called me at 7:14 AM. He goddam informed me that he'd been contacted nine minutes earlier by the High and Mighty Governor of California, Goodwin J. Knight, who's only been occupying that lofty office for little more than two weeks. He was personally instructed by His Eminence in Sacramento that San Bernardino County would goddam provide any and all assistance to one Richard C. Van Loan, whoever the hell he is, in pursuing his investigation of the death of one Frank Havens.

"Now, I gotta admit that this was a goddam first for me, sir. I'm no shrinking violet about these things. I've had pressure put on me before by the politicians"—he pronounced it "pol-ee-tee-shuns"—"but never like this, and never so blatant, goddam it. I don't know how you get so goddam much pull, and I'll tell you straight out, sir, I don't goddam like it, neither.

"But I do what I'm told, so here's the goddam file on Mr. Havens, which *I*, at least, regard as a closed book. The man goddam committed suicide, pure and simple, although I can't label it that way publicly. We're calling it a goddam accident here, and it'll stay that way, too. You'll goddam sign on the dotted line for this, Mr. Van Loan, and you'll goddam return these papers to me when you're done with them. *¿Comprende, amigo?*"

I just smiled and nodded and scrawled an illegible signature on the form that the officer shoved in front of me.

"Thanks a whole bunch," I said on the way out.

"Yeah, swell," came the reply.

My second stop was a dingy office building a few blocks away. The elevator was broken—probably always *had* been broken—so I walked up three flights of stairs and down a corridor, peering at the chipped gold paint on each glass-topped wood door. When I reached the sign that said, "Lazarus N. O'Riley, Investigations," I walked in.

"I've got an appointment," I told the receptionist.

"Mr. Van Loan?" she asked, and when I agreed, buzzed O'Riley's office and then motioned towards the inner sanctum.

"What can I do for you?" the private dick inquired.

He was a slightly hunched man in his mid-thirties, wearing a visor and the pinched look of someone who's seen too many tragedies.

"I've got a problem, O'Riley," I responded, "and you come highly recommended."

"Oh, who by?" the investigator asked.

"Sean Hugh McCarty, for one."

"R-really," the PI sputtered, coughing once or twice. He reached back and grabbed a flask, tilting it backwards to take a swig. "Uh, yes, and just how would you have known Mr. McCarty?"

"I once helped save Mr. McCarty and several others from having their asses fried, so to speak, in an incident involving the New York Gaming Board."

"Uh, yes, I seem to recall a little something of the sort." The man cleared his throat again. "Of course, that was some time ago, Mr. Van Loan. Mr. McCarty, well, he never knew exactly who'd been responsible for his extrication from a slight embarrassment regarding, uh, what was the amount again?"

"A cool quarter million. It was gambled away by one Riley Lazarus McCarty, but of course, you were the one implicated, weren't you, since you covered the bets for the track."

"What could I do?" he mumbled. "He was my older brother, after all."

"Yes, and quite willing to let you and your sibling Patrick take the fall for him."

"Very well, Mr. Van Loan: I'm in your debt. What can I do for you now, sir?"

"A newspaperman named Frank Havens died in mysterious circumstances on Monday evening in an unincorporated portion of San Bernardino County, halfway between San Bernardino and Redlands. I need to know whether he'd made any recent withdrawals in cash from his bank account, and also background information on his financial and professional connections. I want to find any and all irregularities in his situation. Havens was hit by a train. I further need to locate and interview the engineer, plus any investigating officers on the scene, both police and railroad."

"Uh, that would require a significant amount of time and effort on my part, Mr. Van Loan."

"Expense is no object, although you'll overcharge me at your peril, O'Riley. You can reach me care of the Hot Springs Resort. I want regular progress reports."

"Uh, yes, sir, I'll get on it right away, sir." He coughed once more. "Umm, we usually expect a retainer in such circumstances."

"My retainer is my word," I replied, slamming my business card on the desk in front of him. "That and my knowledge of...."

"Uh, yes, of course, sir."

The man tried to smile, but failed. One side of his mouth went up, the other down. It was almost comical to watch.

"Uh, yes, I'll phone you this evening, sir."

"Excellent!" I agreed.

After lunching at the Seven Seas Café on Court Street, I ordered Tigre back to Redlands again, where he left me at an old red brick office on State Street. I walked into a jewelry store and asked to see the owner, one Nathanaël Emerson Zohn.

"How can I help you, sir?" the bespectacled jeweler queried.

He wore a vest and suspenders and baggy pants. A gold pocket watch peeked at me out of his coat.

"I'm a friend of Cullen de Loos. I believe he called?"

"Of course, sir," Zohn said.

"I want some information on Mr. Frank Havens," I indicated, "how he was regarded, his financial situation, his friends and enemies, anything you can tell me."

"Hmm," the jeweler stated. "You understand, sir, that I wouldn't repeat such things to just anyone. I owe Mr. de Loos a large favor, and this inquiry will finally satisfy it."

"That's between you and Mr. de Loos," I noted.

"Very well, sir. Mr. Havens was relatively new to the area, having arrived just two years ago, although his daughter, Mrs. Rowlings, has lived here for some time, five years or more. He bought *The Redlander*, which had been long losing ground to the *Facts*, and redesigned it, adding photos and features and all kinds of new things. Made it work again.

"Of course, Redlands is a very conservative town, always has been. Some folks didn't like his new-fangled ideas and regarded him as an upstart. All of them, however, came to appreciate the man. When you actually met him, he was friendly and open and perfectly charming.

"He loved to play golf, but wasn't very good at it. He was diabetic, and couldn't eat anything with sugar in it. He never was late with his bills, or I would have heard. Always paid cash, never used credit. His wife was younger than he was, and that created a stir at first, but she was well-liked too.

33

"They bought the old Twin Pines Rancho out near San Timoteo Canyon, so I didn't really see all that much of her. They belonged to Saint Picardus Episcopal Church in town. He became an Elk and a Moose, and also joined the Chamber of Commerce."

"What about his adult daughter?"

"Oh, you mean Mrs. Rowlings?" Zohn asked. "She has a pretty solid reputation, that one, certainly better than her husband's."

"Indeed?"

"Well, they say that Dr. Rowlings goes off occasionally on week-long binges, mostly at the Hot Springs Resort. He was in such bad shape on one occasion that he had to be dried out at a sanitarium. He loves betting on the horses, and spends time each season at Santa Anita; sometimes Mr. Havens would join him there. He runs up large tabs, but always manages to pay them off. He and his wife live very well indeed. They have a house up on Smiley Heights, and entertain local society quite frequently. The rumor mill suggests that he's had an occasional dalliance on the side. And further deponent saith not."

"That helps considerably. Thank you, Mr. Zohn," I replied.

I wandered outside and approached the driver's window.

"Tigre, I'm going to walk down the street to another appointment. Wait here for me, please."

A half block away on Fifth Street, I entered a doorway and trod the stairs up to a second-floor office. "Dr. Kenneth J. Rowlings" was emblazoned in gold on the door.

The nurse-receptionist looked up as I entered: "Yes?"

She was a dippy blonde who reminded me of Marilyn Monroe, the young *ingénue* who was sweeping Hollywood these days. Her nails and lips had an orange glow about them, as if she wanted to set the world on fire. Her brittle yellow hair was swept up in a mound and topped with a funny little green nurse's cap. She had a high, squeaky voice, like a hopped-up mouse.

"I'm Mr. Van Loan," I said. "I'd like to see the doctor."

"You have an 'pointment?"

She scrunched her hands up towards her face, meticulously examining her fingertips for flaws.

"No, but I'll wait."

"Have a seat then. Over there."

Gad. She just had to point, didn't she?

A half hour later I heard my name called, and set aside the *Life Magazine* I'd been reading. It featured a piece on the ultra-conservative Earl Warren, who had just been confirmed as Chief Justice of the U.S. Supreme Court.

"Van!" the physician announced as I entered his examination room. "Something wrong?"

"No," I stated. "I just wanted to ask you a few questions about Frank."

"Of course, of course. This is a terrible time for all of us."

"I understand that Mr. Havens had diabetes. I assume you treated him for it."

"Indeed," Rowlings responded. "He had to take regular shots of insulin. Either I or Muriel or Cyndi administered them, since he was so squeamish about injecting himself. I also worked with Cyndi to eliminate as much sugar as I could from his diet. She always fixed him very nutritious meals. I think she kept him alive and active in more ways than one."

"Other than that, how was Frank's health?"

"For a man of eighty, he was still pretty spry," the doctor commented. "He suffered from mild hypertension. It often goes along with the other. He didn't seem to have too many aches and pains, not like some of the elderly. He was thin, but that was a good thing, really. Of course, the diabetes might have killed him in the end. It's usually progressive, and often leads to congestive heart failure."

"What about his mental state?"

"Well, I'm not really qualified medically to comment on something like that," the physician noted, "although it seemed to me he'd been a little depressed recently, and perhaps not as sharp as usual. I don't know the reason. Cyndi might have a better idea."

"Enough to take his own life?"

"Who knows? We're all mysteries to ourselves when it comes right down to it. We all do things we can't explain."

"Did he have a problem with alcohol?"

"No, not at all," Rowlings indicated.

"What about you? I've heard stories...."

"Who from? Look, Van, sure, I occasionally indulge myself—don't we all?—but I never lose control, ever. I'm always there for my patients. I can't afford not to be. I've spent years building up this practice, and I sure as hell don't intend to piss it all away now."

"You supposedly spent time in a sanitarium."

"That's a lie! Who the hell's making these accusations?"

"I'm not at liberty to say," I stated. "Why did you move out here in the first place?"

Rowlings was looking very uncomfortable by this point.

"Well, you already know the reason, Van. We wanted to get away from things back east. The winters were always so bad on Long Island. And Muriel, well, she was a bit sweet on you, you know, and she felt she had to put some distance between you. So we relocated, and this place has been good to us. Frank was close to Muriel, so when he retired, he and Cyndi pulled up roots and joined us."

Then he changed the subject.

"You'll be at the funeral tomorrow?"

"Of course," I replied.

"Afterwards, we're inviting everyone over to the ranch for a feast. That's what Frank would have wanted: people celebrating his life, not crying crocodile tears over his passing."

"I don't think grieving about a good man's loss is a waste of time," I stated.

"I'm not saying that it is," the doctor indicated, "but there's such a thing as grieving too much. The man's dead. Let's celebrate all of the positive things he did while he was alive. We have a saying in California: if you're handed a sack of lemons, make some lemonade."

"Lemonade, huh?" I muttered, shaking my head. Was *that* all the man could say about his patron?

"Doctor Rowlings!"

The nurse-receptionist poked her glowing little head through the doorway and smiled, pursing her lips at the physician.

"Your three o'clock is here."

"I have a patient waiting," Kenneth noted. "I'll see you at the service *mañana*."

"Of course," I agreed.

I ambled back to the Ford and took my seat in the rear

I asked Tigre: "Do you know anyone who works at the Hot Springs Hotel?"

"*Sí, señor*," came the response. "My cousin's cousin, Goliat Geranio, he does many, many things for them, and he will tell me everything you want to know for a *dólar*—and for a few *dólares* more, *señor*, I can open many more doors there and many more mouths. Always, the leettle people, they are so hungry."

"I want you to ask him about a man named Dr. Kenneth Rowlings," I stated. "He supposedly spent some time there. But I don't want anyone to know who's asking questions except for you and me. *¿Comprende?*"

I pulled out my wallet and liberated a hundred-dollar bill, flipping it over the seat.

"Oh, *sí, señor*," the driver responded, "with thees I could make even the dogs on the street bark out their *secretos*."

"Then please do so," I ordered.

That evening I received the first of my verbal reports from Laz O'Riley.

"That publisher of yours was very well regarded in Redlands," he noted. "People are sure sorry he's gone."

"I knew that much already," I stated.

"Kind of a strange bloke, though, if you know what I mean," he continued. "Had his fingers in a lot of different pies. I need to do some more digging to see if it means anything."

"The more you dig, the more I'll pay," I indicated.

"That's what I'm counting on," he said.

I hung up the phone.

Then I looked through the papers that Betty, Frank's secretary, had forwarded me by courier. They covered the short and nondescript career of one John Nemo, typesetter. They told me nothing new, however.

I yawned and called "Room Service," ordering a salad and a beer.

It had been a long but productive day.

V.

"I KNOW WHAT YOU THINK!"
▲

Death makes equal the high and the low.
—John Heywood
▼

REDLANDS, CALIFORNIA
SATURDAY, 24 OCTOBER 1953

Saint Picardus Episcopal Church was located on Fern Street in Redlands, and it was there that the friends and family of Frank Septimus Havens gathered at nine the next morning to pay their final respects. Although he had arrived in the city just two years earlier, the publisher had everywhere been respected for his honor, his kindness, and his ability.

I was included in the family group at the front of the church. All of the remaining seats were taken before the funeral began, with the overflow crowding out the front and side doors. The mass lasted about ninety minutes, and the homily given by Father Theophrastus Levine was simple but moving.

"We will soon walk the path that Frank Havens has just taken," the priest intoned. "We must soon account to the Maker of All Things for our actions and inactions here on earth. I have no doubt whatever that Frank will be waiting to greet us at the Gates of Heaven, each and every one, giving all of us a 'haven' for our eternal rest."

I personally doubted the minister's *pronunciamento*, but then, I've sent too damned many men to their just rewards over the years, whatever those were—and I'm no wiser about such things than anyone else. All I know is that the hells these men had created in the here and now still lingered for the innocents whose lives they'd so casually disrupted. Frank was the counterbalance to such thoughtless evil.

I found myself reflecting on everything that the man had done for me over the decades—and for so many others. He'd quite literally saved my life and soul in the years immediately following my return from the Western Front in the First World War. When I'd despaired of ever finding peace again, of purging from my memory the scenes of death and destruction and suffering, he'd given me a purpose once more. He'd seen something in me that I hadn't even realized myself. He'd restored my

38

soul. For that alone, not to mention the many years I'd basked in the light of his continuing support and friendship, I could never, ever repay him. That fact had driven me to become an avenger, a restorer, and a redresser of sins, mine as well as others'.

When the mass was finished and we began to wend our way back to the sunshine and warmth, I suddenly heard my name called, and turned to find Dastrie Lee Underhill standing there on the church steps, all fresh and young and radiant in basic black. Black suited her very well indeed, as did her sparkling green eyes.

"I wondered if you'd be here," I said.

"Well, Daddy's in no shape to travel," she indicated, "so I'm representing both the family and the force. Is Frank being interred locally?"

"Muriel said that he wanted to be cremated, with his ashes scattered on the ranch near the tomb of an old pioneer who's buried there. That'll happen sometime next week, I guess. Cyndi would have preferred a more traditional burial, I think, but she was overruled.

"Right now, though, we're all going over to Twin Pines for a luncheon-*cum*-wake. You're certainly welcome to ride along—if you dare!"

"Why, Mr. Van Loan! Is that an offer?"

"Just lending a hand," I said, smiling at her slight impertinence.

"Then I graciously and gratefully accept," she stated, giving me her arm.

Before we left the church, however, I went over and hugged Cyndi and Muriel, once more offering my support, and telling them that I'd help in any way that I could.

While Dastrie and I waited patiently for Tigre to appear, Father Levine made his rounds of the family, one by one, earnestly expressing his condolences.

"Our Lord will watch over you and ease your sorrow," he rumbled. "He will…."

There was a loud bang and the priest suddenly opened his eyes very wide. I don't know if Frank was waiting for him at the Pearly Portals or not, but Father Theophrastus soon had his opportunity to find out for himself. He fell forward into my arms, shot once through the heart.

"Get down!" I ordered Dastrie, who'd been standing right next to the murdered man.

But no more bullets were fired at any of us.

This time we experienced the querulous questioning of the ever-ready Redlands Police Department, a rather provincial organization that hadn't a clue how to solve anything more complicated than a daylight dog-snatching. I swear that the officer who interrogated me was the spitting image of Buster Keaton.

Again, though, I could tell them nothing, and neither could Dastrie Underwood. We were finally released two hours later.

"A very sad time, *señor*," Tigre said, holding the car door open for us.

"Very," I agreed.

Dr. Rowlings insisted that Frank's wake proceed as scheduled, so we formed a procession of automobiles that crawled out of Redlands on Highway 99 at a tortoise's pace. Dastrie and I had very little to say on the first stage of that trip. Death has a way of stealing one's eloquence.

"How did you extricate yourself from that difficulty in New York?" I finally asked, breaking the silence.

"I just, um, made a phone call," she replied, frowning briefly.

I'd wondered for some time about my dear Miss Underhill's official or unofficial connections, but had never bothered to exert myself sufficiently to unravel them.

"And they just let you go?" I pressed.

"Yes, they just let me go," she acknowledged. "I understand you have a little problem here yourself."

"As you've seen," I replied. "And I've been asked by the family to investigate Frank's death. No one thinks that it was suicide."

"What do *you* think?" she asked.

"I don't know enough yet to make a judgment," I replied. "The man I knew would never have taken his own life, except under extraordinary circumstances—but I'm not really sure yet what the circumstances might have been in this case. Want to help?"

"Of course," she replied. "I don't need to get back for another week or two."

We agreed that she would relocate from the California Hotel in San Bernardino to the Hot Springs Resort. But by then we were approaching Twin Pines Rancho. Everyone crowded into the main house, talking, talking, talking about the murder of Father Levine. Those of us who were utterly tired of all the killing escaped the gossip and slopped over onto the veranda out back.

"What a beautiful sight," Dastrie mused, idly handing me a drink while gazing at the ridge on the other side of the valley.

"I wonder what Cyndi's going to do with the place now that Frank's gone," I replied. "It's a lot for her to manage by herself. Keeping it going has to be very costly and time-consuming."

At that moment Kenneth asked for everyone's attention, so we went back into the house again.

"A toast," he offered, "to the memory of Frank Havens."

"To Frank Havens," we all intoned.

"Frank saved a lot of us here from ourselves, and I was no exception," the physician continued. "I'd just established my practice on Long

Island when I met Muriel, and Frank, he took care of me in so many ways. He encouraged his friends to become my patients, and when Arnie and I decided to come out west, he lent us the money. He was always watching out for us. I'll miss his lively humor and 'frank' commentary (a wee joke, folks!). I'll miss our trips to Santa Anita (neigh!). I'll miss our weekly chess games with my 'mate.' Here's to ya, Frank!"

"Arnie?" Dastrie whispered in my ear.

"That's what he calls her," I hissed back.

Then Muriel bussed him on the cheek. She'd changed in some way that I really couldn't fathom. She looked harder to me, a little worn around the edges; and the lines surrounding her eyes and lips seemed almost like canyons in the slant of the stark fall sunlight. This had been a rough time for her, and it was obvious to me that the hard times had been going on here for more than just a week.

Frank's other friends began making their own public testimonials. I wanted to speak out myself, but I couldn't, not here and not now. Everything that had passed between us was private history—and it had to stay that way.

The party or celebration or whatever lingered on for another three hours, but Dastrie and I finally bade our farewells and headed to the car. Tigre was patiently waiting for us.

"What's this?" Dastrie asked, as she slid over the seat.

She held up another one of those damnable cards.

"It looks just like the note from the restaurant," she added. "THE PHANTOM'S PHANTOM. I KNOW WHAT YOU THINK! How very odd."

I sat down beside her. Then she saw the expression on my face.

"This isn't the second one, is it, Richard? There've been more!"

"There have," I admitted, "many more."

"So who's sending you these things—The Phantom Detective?"

"I don't believe so," I indicated. "I think it's a copycat."

"But why?"

"It apparently started with Frank—and now he's dead," I said. "The connection is there, if it's anywhere."

She looked at me with her head cocked sideways, as if seeing me for the very first time. Her eyes narrowed, just for a moment, and I could see the brains in that beautiful head cooking overtime.

"It's *you*, isn't it?" she finally stated. "*You're* the Phantom! Jeez! It all fits, everything I've ever heard, all the speculations, all the stories, the link with Frank, where you live, everything. *You're* the Phantom, Richard!"

I sighed.

"Even if that were true," I countered, "it wouldn't make the slightest difference now. The Phantom's retired—permanently. He was the product of a world now dead, a world destroyed by the Second World

41

War and everything that followed. All that he was is gone—and maybe it's good riddance too."

"I don't think so," she said, "and neither do you. He was an icon, Richard. He was somebody you could look up to. When I was a kid, he was all we talked about. All of us wanted to wear that mask. All of us wanted to become The Phantom Detective."

"Dastrie, whoever's doing this to me—whoever did it to Frank—isn't going to stop until he's caught. He's targeting all my friends. You were standing right next to Levine when he was killed. The bullet might have been intended for you. This isn't a game, Dastrie, at least not for us. If you get in the way, he'll take you out, just like that."

"I'm quite, quite capable of protecting myself, Mr. Van Loan," she responded coolly, "as you've already seen."

"Just don't underestimate him," I warned. "This man is very clever and resourceful and dangerous, and he seems to be everywhere. I can't find him and I can't shake him. He's like an old dog that just won't let go."

"*I'll* help you find him," Dastrie blurted out. "Together we can locate him!"

"Yes," I admitted, "that's what I'm afraid of."

Later that afternoon, after we'd resettled Dastrie at the Hot Springs Hotel, I received a second phone report from Laz O'Riley.

"I've located the engineer," he said. "He'll see you tomorrow after church, for a 'C' note and assurances that what he says will stay private."

"Fair enough," I responded.

"He lives in Colton," the PI noted, giving me the address. "He said he'd meet you there at eleven."

"Call him and let him know I'm coming. Then I want to see you here at three. Oh, and I need a muscle man, if you can find one."

"Got the perfect candidate," he noted, "Zinc Molrad. He's big and agile and handy with several different kinds of weapons. I've used him before, and he's always reliable."

"See if he's available," I instructed, "and bring him with you tomorrow afternoon."

"The railroad dick can meet you at the resort Monday morning, say, about ten o'clock? He'll want a bit more greasing than the engineer. Same privacy concerns, of course."

"Not a problem," I stated. "Please arrange it."

"I'm still trying to pry loose one of the cops who worked the scene, but it's going to be tough. Ole 'Willie Boy' has told 'em to stay clear of you."

"I rather thought that he'd do something like that," I said. "Any suggestions on how we can put some additional pressure on Mr. Jardine?"

"Well, they say he likes to prowl the cat houses down on lower 'D' Street," O'Riley replied. "He's even a little rough at times with the kittens. I can probably persuade one of the fair ladies to rat him out, if you can buy her way into a new life somewhere else."

"Consider it done."

"Will do, boss. I like the way you work. See ya *mañana*."

An idea was percolating in my mind. A lone crusader wasn't enough anymore. Alone, I could no longer fight the many-tentacled monsters of crime: there were just too many of them, and they were too well organized and financed. To act against the concomitant evils of corrupt officialdom and the oily underworld, I needed a multi-pronged approach. I needed the talents of many different individuals joining together in a dedicated group of crime-fighters.

I broached the notion to Dastrie Underhill over dinner.

"Well, you have the makings of the thing already," she noted with her usual astute evaluation. "The people who've come together in this case will provide you with the nucleus of an organization, at least on the West Coast. Then you just build a structure around them, bringing in more specialists as needed in the future. You make them employees and more than employees. You dedicate and inspire and energize them in the same way that you've dedicated yourself, Richard.

"I know who you are," she added, smiling at me.

"That's what the first note stated," I indicated.

"Well, it's pretty obvious when you think of it," she responded. "You can do this thing, Richard. You're the one person who knows what has to be done, and who has the ability and the knowledge and the money to actually accomplish the task. Once started, the organization will survive and prosper on its own.

"I can help you. I can do some of the things that you can't. And that's true of Lazarus O'Riley and your driver as well, from what little you've told me. They all have their own contributions to make, even Liz, your office manager. One by one, we can find the individuals who will fit into the mosaic and strengthen it.

"Let me aid you, Richard."

"What about your job, whatever that is?" I asked, grinning slightly in return.

"There's nothing there that I want to keep," Dastrie stated. "But I have connections in the government that might prove useful to us in the future, so I wouldn't want to sever my ties entirely. That's true of everyone we've talked about this evening."

Our waiter appeared and I signed for our tab.

"I've asked Laz O'Riley to meet me here tomorrow at three," I said. "I'd like you to be there as well, not only to review what we know about these cases, but also to discuss some of the things that you've proposed."

"I'm happy to be part of this," the young woman replied. "I'd *love* to do this, Richard."

"Then let's begin," I said.

VI.

"I KNOW HOW YOU FEEL!"
▲

I said to Heart, "How goes it?" Heart replied:
"Right as a Ribstone Pippin!" But it lied.
—Hilaire Belloc
▼

COLTON AND SAN BERNARDINO, CALIFORNIA
SUNDAY, 25 OCTOBER 1953

I've never been much of a church-going man. It's not because I haven't any faith in the Almighty, whoever He is, but I've just never been much of a joiner. I belonged to several official organizations in the Big Apple to maintain my supposed place in society, although even there I've cut my ties to many of them in recent years, following my "retirement" from active life. I always figured that any religious body that would allow a rampant sinner like me to become part of their congregation was no group that I really wanted to join. I can hum along quite well from the back pews, thank you very much.

But as I've aged, I've also come to realize that I won't go on forever. I think it was the confrontation with the Jojoba Gang in Nopales that finally put some terminal punctuation on the consideration of my own mortality. Up to that point, I'd never been particularly reflective, but spending three weeks in the hospital has a remarkable way of concentrating one's attention. I suddenly knew that I could just as easily have died from the wounds that I'd received—and that no one would have much cared about my passing, even Muriel Rowlings.

So maybe Dastrie was right. Maybe it was time to try something new with my life. The old methods no longer worked. If I was now an old dog, I'd have to learn some additional tricks if I wanted to survive.

I decided to start the new regime right away.

I arose as usual at six, and went through my routine of exercises, contemplation, and purging, trying to prepare myself for a new day. Since I had some time to kill, I went searching for the spa at the hot springs attached to the back of the hotel, and soaked there in the steaming mineral waters for an hour, allowing the heat to fully penetrate my bones. I felt very relaxed and refreshed afterwards.

45

Then I dressed, ate a quick snack, and met Tigre at the Hotel entrance. I mentioned the three o'clock meeting in my room, and asked him to join us.

"You want *me* there, *señor*?" he posed.

"You're part of my team now," I replied. "I can use your help."

"I weell follow you anywhere, Meester Van Loan," he stated.

It took us an hour to find the railroad engineer in Colton.

The latter was a community located quite literally on the other side of the tracks from San Bernardino. Both cities were heavily dependent on a trio of major rail companies—Santa Fe, Southern Pacific, and Union Pacific—whose main lines into Los Angeles passed right through the two communities on their way to the Cajon Pass or Palm Springs. All had major servicing and sorting yards located in the immediate vicinity.

Harry Lee Crosby was the driver's name. He lived on Vallejo Avenue in the northern, non-Hispanic part of town. He might have been sixty years of age, with a potbelly and unshaven face and mop of gray hair flopping over his forehead. There were dark circles under his eyes.

"I can still see the guy," he mumbled. "The first accident I ever had in forty years with the 'road. The very first one in all that time! And this old coot, he just stalls his car on the track and then opens the door and stumbles out and staggers, like he was drunk or something—or maybe he just didn't know what he was doing, I dunno—but he wanders down the track right at me; and I couldn't stop in time, even though I was only going about ten, and I ran him over and then hit his car too.

"God, I can still see his face when I close my eyes, the horror in his eyes as he realized he was about to die. He didn't want to die, I swear, and I told the cops that too, but they didn't believe me. They found a note or something in his pocket, they said, but I heard one of them talking about it afterward, you know, while I was waiting, and it was nothing, just a message to his daughter telling her to do the right thing, and they thought because of that he committed suicide.

"He was afraid, I tell you, and he didn't want to die, but he just didn't know what to do somehow, like he didn't have total control of his body, he was moving in jerks and fits and such like a puppet on a string. God, I can still see his face staring at me!"

"Where did this happen?" I asked.

"The line services the orange growers and a packing house on San Bernardino Avenue. It runs along the west side of the street. The tracks aren't in very good shape, so we have a speed limit of fifteen MPH. He was stalled right where the line crosses Alabama Street."

"Did you spot anyone else hanging around?"

"Well, sir…well, it was getting dark already. I may have seen a shadow or something over by the packing house, but I'm really not sure 'bout that." He shook his head. "That face, God, I can still see his face!"

"What direction were you going?"

"I was traveling south towards Alabama Street."

"What about the car?"

"He'd obviously been driving north on San Bernardino Avenue, and was trying to turn left onto Alabama to go back to Redlands. Like I said, the tracks follow the right-hand edge of the road."

"Wait a minute," I interrupted. "You told me that he opened the door and then staggered towards your engine."

"Yes, sir, that's right."

"But if the auto was pointing west, if it was entering Alabama Street, then the driver would have been on the opposite side of the vehicle, correct?"

Crosby's face turned even grayer than it was.

"You're right," he finally admitted, again shaking his broom of salt-and-pepper hair. "But the thing was just like I said, Mr. Van Loan. The car was stuck on the tracks facing north and west, pointing at the packing house, and he opened the *right* door and stumbled towards me."

"Then who drove him there?"

"I…I really don't know, sir."

And that was all that I could get out of him. I didn't think he'd ever drive an engine again. His confidence was shot all to hell.

We stopped for lunch at Lolita's, a little Mexican restaurant on Baseline Street, and I ordered this absolutely marvelous soup or stew called *cocido*. The bowl was filled to the brim with chunks of beef, slices of fresh corn on the cob, green beans, celery, squash, carrots, potatoes, onions, cactus, and a few other things that I couldn't even identify, served with fresh, warm, thick corn tortillas on the side, and a strongly brewed lager that made one really sit up and take notice.

I decided that I could get used to this.

"You like, *señor*?" Tigre asked.

He was chugging down forks full of something that he called *chipotle con pollo* (or it might have been the other way 'round). I tried the large bite that he offered me, and it just about blew my tongue through the roof of my mouth. It was like eating lava. I hastily downed a glass of water in addition to my beer. The proprietor just chuckled a bit.

"A leetle warm, *señor*?" the man inquired.

I couldn't even respond.

Finally I managed to gasp at Tigre: "H-how can you actually *eat* this stuff?"

"What?" he replied, looking at me in puzzlement, and then finally down at his dish. "Thees? Thees ees nothing, *señor*. In México, ha, ha, ha, in México they serve eet *really* hot!"

God help the Mexicanos, I thought to myself. Still, my *cocido* was superb, and probably fairly good for me too.

That afternoon saw the first meeting of what would eventually become The Phantom Detective Agency.

"Lady and gentlemen," I intoned, when everyone had gathered in the living room of my suite in Room 620 of the Hot Springs Hotel, "I'm pleased to welcome you here. My name is Richard Curtis Van Loan. I was also once known as The Phantom Detective."—collective gasps— "That secret, one that was long maintained between myself and Frank Havens and two other persons, no longer has any importance.

"Still, I caution you that all such secrets can be dangerous to one's health, both individually and collectively. The workings of this organization must be kept utterly confidential, lest you also be targeted by The Phantom's Phantom."

I then introduced each of the attendees—Dastrie Lee Underhill, Tigre Durán, Laz O'Riley, Nate Zohn (whom I'd invited earlier in the day), and Zinc Molrad (he looked like a football player, with no neck visible under his slouched hat)—and reviewed the series of occurrences that had led to this day. I also told them what I knew about Frank Havens's apparent murder.

"These two events are tied together in some way," I stated, "but how and why and to what extent we don't yet know. We shouldn't at this juncture assume that both crimes were committed by the same individual or individuals. Questions, anyone?"

"How do we proceed?" Dastrie asked.

"I envision an undercover crime-fighting organization in which each of you would become active participants, if you agree. I'd put all of you on salaries that would far exceed anything that you could possibly earn elsewhere, and I would require nothing less than the best that you have to offer, plus an absolute devotion to the cause and to the group as a whole.

"I'd eventually add similarly minded individuals in New York and other locations. We'd use your PI license, Laz, as partial cover for our activities in California, in addition to the various corporate shells that I'd create here and elsewhere. We'd cooperate with the law where such cooperation was possible or desirable, but always we'd have the ultimate goal of eradicating major crime and criminals and criminous conspiracies wherever we found them—and if any government officials were involved, we wouldn't hesitate to expose them as well.

"None of it would be easy, but I have the wherewithal, folks, to accomplish the task, both financially and in every other way. You have an opportunity to get in on the ground floor of an enterprise that will require of you everything that you are. It'll consume you just as it's consumed me, but you'll be grateful to be part of it."

"I'm in," Dastrie replied without hesitation.

"*Sí*. I will do thees also," Tigre said.

"Would I be allowed to continue my business as well?" Nate inquired.

"I'd insist on it," I responded. "We all need to maintain our respective covers, at least to some degree. Also, each of you has specific skills and connections to other worlds that would be potentially useful to our new organization."

"Very well," he continued, "I agree."

"I work for pay," Zinc stated. "You pay, I work, simple as that."

Everyone was now looking at Lazarus O'Riley.

"What *is* this?" he sputtered, shrinking down into his chair. "Look, Van Loan, I did you a favor, OK, in return for the one you did me, by agreeing to take you on as a client. I didn't sign up for anything else."

"No, you didn't," I agreed. "And all I ask now is that you think about it, Laz. But if you opt out, you still have to keep your mouth shut, for reasons that we've already discussed. Agreed?"

"Yeah," he said with a frown, "but I ain't happy with the notion."

"I didn't and don't guarantee your happiness," I indicated. "Now, do any of you have anything else to report?"

"Yeah," Laz stated sitting up straight again. "That son-in-law of Havens, Dr. Rowlings, he didn't leave New York cuz he wanted to. Something else was going on there. I'm not sure what it was yet, but it was buried pretty damn deep."

"Find out what you can," I ordered. "If Frank was deliberately killed, there are just two possibilities: first, that he was eliminated by The Phantom's Phantom, this mysterious agent who's been harassing me this past week, and who harassed him for a month before that; or second, that the reason was more personal, rooted somewhere in his family or professional life. I want to know everything that there is to know about his intimate connections."

"Well, like I told you before," Laz said, "the man had lots of ties to various businesses even after he'd retired. I mean, he was still serving on the boards of a dozen corporations, and he had indirect links to many other organizations. It's impossible to unravel them all."

"Do what you can," I stated. "Other comments, anyone?"

"We need a name," Dastrie indicated.

"Suggestions?" I posed to the group.

At that moment there was a sharp rap on the door. I motioned Zinc to hide himself in the bedroom and cover us, before strolling across the carpet and yelling, "Yes?"

"Telegram for Mr. Van Loan," came the faint response.

"Just a moment, please."

I cautiously cracked the opening and peered out. A skinny little kid in a funny uniform was standing there, holding a small envelope in one hand and shifting back and forth on his feet, as if he had to pee really badly.

I gave him a quarter and took the message.

"What is it?" Dastrie wanted to know, as I sat back down in my chair.

I popped the flap open and quickly scanned the contents.

"Damn!" I exclaimed. "Roscoe Wallace, one of my employees, has been mugged and killed in Central Park while trying to catch a bus."

Another tap-tap-tapping sounded on my chamber door. My head jerked back to the aperture. This time it was Dastrie who answered the call.

"Wait!" I shouted, but she had already opened the door and taken the message.

It was my turn to ask, "What?"

"Just another telegram," she replied, handing it to me.

I popped the flap and read it out loud to the group.

"I KNOW HOW YOU FEEL! STOP." the note said.

It was signed, "T.P.P."

"This isn't funny anymore," I noted.

And with that we adjourned.

VII.

"I KNOW WHY YOU ACT!"

▲

She bid me take life easy, as the grass grows on the weirs;
But I was young and foolish, and now am full of tears.
—William Butler Yeats

▼

San Bernardino, California
Monday, 26 October 1953

Early the next morning, I had the hotel desk call the long-distance operator for me. It took her forty-five minutes to establish the connection to New York; she phoned my room when the call finally came through.

"Van Loan Enterprises," Lizzie intoned at the other end of the line.

"It's me," I said. "I want you to add several individuals to the payroll"—I dictated the names, addresses, and amounts, including Lazarus O'Riley (let him turn down the money if he dared!)—"You can list them as consultants for the time being."

"Yes, sir."

"Oh, and give yourself a raise while you're at it, Miss Bordone."

"I already make more money than I can reasonably spend, sir," Lizzie responded. "What else would I buy?"

"That's a question that even a PI would have difficulty answering," I responded.

"However," I continued, "I intend to establish an organization called The Phantom Detective Agency. It should be based in New York and California, with a branch in either San Bernardino or Los Angeles. Please find out what's necessary to accomplish this in both states—licensing requirements, etc. You can report back to me when I return."

"How's your investigation of Mr. Havens's death going, sir?" she asked.

"I have an idea of what happened and why, but I can't prove it yet, Lizzie. I'm waiting for some additional information. I hope to wind things up by the end of the week, though, so please book me a return flight from Los Angeles International for the evening of November First."

"Yes, sir. What's it like out there?"

I told her that Southern California was a perfect paradisiacal paradigm of sunshine and warmth.

"Well, it's cold and damp here in New York," she stated. "Please bring some of that good weather back to us, boss."

"I'll try," I said.

My meeting with Robert Zimmerman (the railroad detective) was scheduled for ten, so I had time for another soak and a light breakfast in the hotel snack room. Apples were coming into season in California, and I was hoping, I guess, that an apple a day would keep my Phantom at bay. It hadn't worked thus far!

I figured that my harasser had just been toying with me. He didn't want me dead—he could have accomplished that on several occasions. No, he wanted to humiliate me and embarrass me and even scare me, he wanted to see me crack, maybe he even wanted to put me in jail. I thought back on my long career as a crime-fighter, and I knew that I'd made a good many enemies along the way. I'd attacked and wounded and maimed and killed hundreds of vilely vicious villains, and I wasn't the least bit sorry that I had—but some of those crooks had survived, and some had friends and family who'd survived, and their number was quite simply legion.

Without much more information, I wouldn't be able to determine who was lurking behind the "The Phantom's Phantom." I had to lure the bastard into the open. And the best way to do *that*, I thought, was just to continue with my normal routine. It would infuriate him.

Zimmerman was a big guy who clearly enjoyed his status as a semi-official cop. He had no authority whatever outside his company's railroad yards, offices, and tracks, but what little he possessed he was determined to flaunt. I strongly suspected that his uniform was a tad gaudier than regulations permitted. He sported a gold-braided cap that would have looked good on the local chief of police, and he carried a pearl-handled six-shooter on his right hip that gave him the appearance of an old-time gunslinger—an image that was utterly ruined by the yellow-striped pants.

"I'm Sergeant Zimmerman," he intoned.

He entered my room and plopped down in an overstuffed armchair.

I doubted if the title was official either, but I played along.

"Well, sergeant," I said, "what can you tell me about the death of Mr. Havens?"

I dropped a couple of Ben Franklins on the table in front of him.

The railroad dick folded the money and slipped it into his shirt pocket, and then pulled out a notepad and flipped it open with an ostentatious fluttering of the pages.

52

"Ahem," he muttered (yes, he actually said, "Ahem!"). "I arrived on the scene about 7:45 that evening, Monday, October the Nineteenth.

"The San Bernardino Sheriff's Department already had half a dozen officers investigating the crash. Roadblocks had been established on both streets. An ambulance was present, but it was obvious that the victim was already dead, probably from the very moment he'd been struck by the train. The engineer was almost incoherent, but we managed to establish the sequence of events without difficulty. He was obviously not to blame.

"The facts are these:

"A single-unit switching diesel pulling five boxcars had plowed into a 1951 Buick at the corner of Alabama and San Bernardino, severely damaging the vehicle. The impact took place between 7:00 and 7:15 PM. The driver of the automobile had exited prior to the impact, but was himself run over and killed. His body had to be pulled from beneath the engine; it was badly chewed up. Identity was established through a wallet found on the man's clothing.

"It appeared that Mr. Havens had been attempting to turn left onto Alabama Street from San Bernardino Avenue, and had stalled his vehicle on the tracks. The railroad line parallels the road here but is not actually part of it, and the depth of the track is significant except when it crosses the pavement. Mr. Havens had apparently overshot the corner slightly and put the right front wheel of his automobile onto a section of rail that was too deep for him to traverse. He hadn't been able to extricate himself. He'd tried abandoning the vehicle when the train approached, but had panicked in the dark and run in the wrong direction."

"By all accounts, sergeant," I noted, "the diesel was traveling south along San Bernardino Avenue."

Zimmerman checked his pad again.

"Yes, sir, that's correct."

"And Mr. Havens was turning west onto Alabama Street."

"Yes, sir."

"So why did Mr. Havens exit the right side of the car? The train was rapidly approaching him from that vantage point."

"Uh,…"

Zimmerman flipped the pages up and down, looking for an answer.

"Well, sir, he committed suicide."

"That's a conclusion after the fact," I noted. "Couldn't he also have been a passenger in the automobile?"

"Well, sir, they found a note stuck in his pocket. Let's see, yes, here it is."—he dictated from his notebook—"'Arnie, please take care of everything for me. I'm so sorry this had to happen. Dad.' This 'Arnie' was a pet name for Mr. Havens's daughter, Mrs. Rowlings."

53

"Was the note dated?" I inquired.

"No, sir."

"Then how do you know that it was a suicide message, or even that it was written at the time of the accident?"

"Uh, well, sir, that's just what it appeared to be to everyone on the scene. I mean, all of the investigators came to the same conclusion. Of course, it wasn't reported that way to avoid scandal. The death is officially listed as an accident. But I informed the company in my report that Mr. Havens took his own life, so that no claim of negligence could be made against the railroad in the future by Mr. Havens's estate."

"I believe there's a citrus packing house on the northwest corner of San Bernardino and Alabama, adjacent to a siding coming off the main track, correct?" I pressed.

Zimmerman looked down at his pad again.

"Yes, sir," he finally rumbled. "The San Bernardino Growers' Association operates a facility there that services the local orange growers."

"Was anyone from the plant present at the time of the accident?"

"Uh, I don't believe so, sir," he responded. "The new crop of navels isn't ripe yet, so the plant is only operating with a skeletal staff during regular business hours. They'd all gone home for the night by the time I'd arrived. There could have been a watchman, I suppose, but I didn't see anybody."

"Were there any cars parked in the dirt lot out back?" I asked.

He paused for moment, and then paged and paged and paged through his notes, before finally looking up at me again.

"I don't know, sir. I'm not sure that anyone actually checked the lot. Many of the emergency vehicles were back there. Everything was focused on the accident itself. I don't see why it's important in any case."

"Well, sergeant," I responded, "if there'd been another vehicle parked behind the packers between 5:00 and 7:15 PM, it's possible that whoever was driving Havens's car could have abandoned it to its fate and departed the scene in the second vehicle."

"But it was suicide, sir. I mean, that's what everyone said," Zimmerman emphasized.

"And you wouldn't question the official version of the events, would you, sergeant?"

"No, sir, why would I?"

"Why indeed," I muttered. "Do you know if this was a special train, or was it regularly scheduled?"

"They ran the same route every night at about that time," he stated.

"The engineer said that Mr. Havens appeared drunk or otherwise incapacitated, and that he was staggering around on the tracks. Did the sheriff's deputies find any sign of alcohol or drugs in the car?"

"An empty bottle was reported, sir," he replied. "One of the officers mentioned a smell of booze on the victim, although, as I said, he was also pretty well cut up."

"What about an autopsy?"

"I don't think one was performed," the railroad cop noted. "Mr. Havens was a prominent local businessman, and no one wanted to drag his family into the dirt. His body was cremated, I believe, at the request of his daughter, Mrs. Rowlings."

"Didn't his wife have a say in the matter?"

"I don't know for sure, sir, although I heard a rumor that she was so broken up by the death that she consented to the disposal of the body before she really understood what was going on—and by then it was too late, of course."

I couldn't get anything else out of him, so I let him go.

Dastrie Underhill then sauntered in from the bedroom, where she'd been lurking at my behest.

"What did you make of that?" I asked. "Is he straight?"

"Not much imagination there," she noted. "I think he reported things as he saw them, but he saw what he was told to see or what he wanted to see, and nothing more. He wasn't looking for anything else. The railroad doesn't want to be held liable for Frank's death. So he followed the lead of the sheriff's deputy in charge of the scene."

"I wonder who that was?" I asked. "You up for a ride?"

"Is that an invitation, sir?" she replied, raising her carefully plucked eyebrows at me in mock humor.

"We need to examine the scene of the crime," I stated, "before we go any further with our investigation."

"I agree," she replied, "and afterwards you can treat me to one of these local cafés you've been raving about."

"It's a deal!" I said, laughing a little at the prospect of getting out again.

I phoned Tigre and asked him to bring the car around.

It was another glorious, gorgeous day in Southern California, with a light Santa Ana breeze blowing down from the San Bernardino Mountains, warming everything with its arid, zephyr-like breath. When we stepped outside, the fresh air and the bright sunshine boosted both our energy and our spirits.

"It's so great to be alive!" Dastrie exclaimed, giggling like a little girl who's found a new doll to cherish. "I love this weather. You should buy a place out here, Richard, and spend every winter in California."

"Maybe I will," I responded.

Then Tigre arrived with the car, and we headed down a winding driveway to the highway. Behind us on the mountainside loomed the great, dangling, gray patch of soil that formed the shape of an arrowhead, an icon that had long been celebrated in local Indian lore. It pointed right down at the top of the hotel, like a giant sword of Damocles.

The main road, the Rim of the World Drive, continued up Waterman Canyon into the mountains, eventually reaching the small communities of Crestline and Lake Arrowhead; but instead we turned left on the highway towards San Bernardino. We soon crossed the dusty, rusty rails of the old trolley that had serviced the resort until 1942, when the power lines had been removed; but the tracks had been left for the train that rumbled daily up to the hot springs south of the spa itself, to cart away tank-loads of the pure mineral waters for rebottling elsewhere.

Rim of the World Drive became Waterman Avenue in San Bernardino, and we followed that street all the way through the city, turning left on Mill and right on Tippecanoe, crossing the bridge over the dry wash of the Santa Ana River, and then left again immediately thereafter onto San Bernardino Avenue. Although we'd skirted the southwest corner of Norton Air Force Base, we found the rest of the area mostly undeveloped, interspersed with the occasional blots of poorly maintained houses and downtrodden businesses.

San Bernardino Avenue was flanked on either side by a long line of skinny palm trees reaching at least eighty feet into the sky, their small clusters of fronds incongruously balancing at the top of narrow, insubstantial poles that looked entirely incapable of supporting the weight. This bizarre vista was the strangest thing that I saw in all of California.

Orange groves crowded each side of the street, cut back slightly on the right-hand side to allow room for the railroad track that flanked the roadway.

"Great place to hide a body," Dastrie noted, nodding at the trees.

She had a rather peculiar way of looking at things.

"What's that?" she asked, pointing at the odd-looking metal contraption poking its shiny head above the orchard.

It reminded me of the alien machine from *The War of the Worlds*.

"Smudge pots," I noted. "They use them in the winter whenever the temperatures fall below freezing. Citrus trees are particularly vulnerable to frost damage."

"*Señor*," Tigre interrupted, "behind us!"

I glanced out the back window and saw a pickup approaching rapidly from the rear. Two heads were visible behind the windshield, bobbing up and down as the truck crunched through the potholes in the pavement. I saw the man on the passenger's side suddenly shove a gun out his open window.

"Step on it!" I ordered, and our car jumped forward down the narrow, two-lane road.

I pushed Dastrie to the floor as the rear window of the Ford was cratered.

"¿Dónde, señor?" the driver yelled.

We'd just passed Alabama and could see the end of San Bernardino Avenue looming in front of us several blocks ahead.

"To Redlands!" I shouted.

Tigre swerved the station wagon right around the corner of Tennessee Street. The truck was almost touching our bumper now.

Another *bang!* another hit, and then the pickup skittered by, just missing a car heading towards us in the opposite direction. The shooter in the pickup tossed a large placard onto the verge of the road as the truck sped off towards town.

"Bastards!" I said, and then ordered Tigre to stop the car.

"Can I come up for air now?" Dastrie inquired, lifting her head above the level of the seat as we coasted to the margin.

I opened the door and got out, trying to catch my breath. Dastrie soon joined me there, and then walked over and picked up the sign.

"Well, will you look at this," she said, holding the thing up where I could read the words painted on its face.

"I KNOW WHY YOU ACT!" it proclaimed.

"This Phantom is becoming a real pain in the ass," I muttered.

"We could have been killed," Dastrie commented.

"I don't think so," I replied. "The intent here was to scare or intimidate us, not to murder or maim."

I tossed the thing back into the weeds.

"We still have a job to do, so let's get on with it," I stated.

We turned around and drove sedately back up Tennessee to San Bernardino, and back again to the corner of Alabama Street, parking in the unpaved lot behind the packing house. In another month or so the place would be swarming with workers and trucks and train cars, but right now a moderately sized crew of about ten men was cleaning, organizing, repairing benches and bins, and generally getting the place ready for the real work that would soon commence.

"I'm looking for the manager," I said.

One of the workers pointed to an office in the far corner of the facility. I went over and pounded on the door.

The chief's name was Arnold Dorsey, a fastidious little twit incongruously dressed to the nines in a tweed coat, brown tie, and vest. Talking to him was like trying to get a response out of the federal government.

"Yes?" he asked.

"Mr. Richards, Incontinental Insurance Group," I stated, flashing a card so quickly that he couldn't see it, "and this is Miss Dastrie. We're investigating the accident that took place on this corner last week."

"Oh, yes, I heard about that," Dorsey replied. "It was terrible."

"Were you or any of your men on duty at that time?" I posed.

"No, sir. Just Jackson."

"Just Jackson?"

"The guard, sir."

"Can I meet this Mr. Jackson?"

"Five o'clock," came the reply.

"Please let him know," I said, "that we'll be back."

Then Dastrie and Tigre and I wandered out to the front of the property, where we examined the section of road and track where the collision had occurred. The wreckage had already been cleaned up, of course, and the bent rail straightened, but you could still see where the car had stalled.

"You'd really have to work to jam this up," Dastrie commented, peering down at the scene.

"Sí, señorita," Tigre added.

He touched my shoulder, pointing to a street sign posted at the corner.

"El automóvil, he would have to go thees way and then that way to reach the hole in *el ferrocarril* without he heets the post."

I saw immediately what he meant. You couldn't reach the place where the Buick had been stuck without actually maneuvering the vehicle into place. It couldn't have happened accidentally, even if the car had been cruising at the grand speed of five MPH.

"This was done deliberately," I stated, and my two companions nodded in agreement.

"There must have been a getaway car," I added, "probably parked behind the packing house—which means that there was at least one other person involved besides Frank and his driver."

"Why didn't the police see this?" Dastrie inquired.

"They didn't want to see it," I replied. "Maybe they were paid not to see it, or perhaps it was just their natural incompetence oozing out once again."

Suddenly a car pulled up to the corner, its little red light flashing, and a sheriff's deputy emerged. I wondered if his name was Rudolph. He sauntered over, his hips swaggering like those of a swank model flouncing down a New York fashion runway.

"Mr. Jardine wants to see you, Van Loan," he intoned, "right now!"

"I think we're done here," I said to my companions. "We'll just follow you downtown, officer."

"You'd better," he replied.

"Or what?" I responded. "You'll arrest me?"

But we were already walking away, and he just stood sputtering at us, not knowing what to say. He'd already exceeded the limit of his instructions.

When we reached the San Bernardino County Courthouse, "Willie Boy" was not a happy camper. He was about to utter the "F" word when noticed the comely female standing by my side.

"Who's she?" he finally posed.

"Dastrie Lee Underhill," she replied. "I'm Mr. Van Loan's private, uh, assistant."

She then smiled sweetly at him with those ruby-red lips. I don't think his heart melted—he didn't have a heart—but something else certainly moved, and it wasn't Mother Earth or Father Time either.

"What can we do for you, sheriff?" I asked.

"Somebody's been mucking about in my private affairs," Jardine muttered under his breath. "Somebody's going to get himself into goddam serious trouble if he's not real careful. San Berdoo ain't no sissy town, Van Loan. We run a tight ship here. Rule No. 1 is this: the captain gets to do what he wants. *¿Comprende?*"

"The captain also goes down with his ship," I noted. "No one's going to be embarrassed if we do things by the book, sheriff, if we all act like reasonable gentlemen. I just want to interview a few of your men about the, uh, accident involving Mr. Havens. I don't intend to point fingers at you or anybody else. My report will be made privately to the family.

"But should I not receive the cooperation that the governor requested on my behalf, not only will he be informed of your intransigence, but certain facts concerning your, uh, very active social life will be leaked to the press. *¿Comprende, amigo?*"

The sheriff cleared his throat several times before pulling out a cigar box. He offered me one—I politely declined, although Dastrie looked interested—before pulling out a Cuban cheroot and snipping off the tip in the quaint little guillotine on his desk. He inhaled and exhaled several long puffs of the pungent smoke, which brought to mind a rendering plant that I'd once encountered in upstate New York while chasing Felix Navidad and his Cuban Cargo Cult.

"OK," he finally stated, "the men you want will be made available to you tomorrow and Wednesday. But you goddam screw this up for me, Van Loan, and governor or not, I'll throw you in the clink so fast you won't know which way your head is spinning. Now get the goddam hell out of my office!"

He looked pointedly at Dastrie, tried to grin, and spat, "Sorry, ma'am."

"That's quite goddam all right. Nice meeting you, sheriff," my companion tossed over her shoulder on the way out. "Maybe I'll come up and see you sometime."

"That was very, very cruel," I noted as we walked out the front of the building, "toying with a grown man like that."

"I've met the type before," she replied. "They like to knock their girls around, just to show us they're 'real' he-men. With a little more information, I could find a way of curbing Lothario's lust."

"I'll think on it," I said. "I may have use of him again."

"You use everyone, Richard, even me," she noted. "I don't mind, of course: it helps keep life interesting."

"Nor should you," I stated.

"Still, I'd appreciate this one favor," she pressed.

"We'll see."

We stopped for a late lunch at El Rebuzno de los Burros, a hole-in-the-wall café located on Court Street, with Tigre joining us.

Dastrie picked up the stained typed menu at the counter.

"What's a 'garbage' *burrito?*" she inquired. "It sounds absolutely disgusting."

"Oh no, *señorita*, ees very good," our driver assured her.

"Richard, I don't know what any of this stuff is," my companion complained. "Maybe I'll just order a salad."

"Try the *tamales*, *señorita*," Tigre suggested. "Ees mild."

"I'm game," she said, putting down the ragged sheet.

"I'll order the chicken *fajitas*," I stated.

And Tigre ate something he called *chicharrones*, which really *did* look disgusting.

"What are they?" I wanted to know.

"The, uh, the peeg skin, *señor*."

"I've never seen a pig that looked like that," Dastrie observed.

"The skin, eet ees fried," Tigre responded. *"¡Bueno!"*

And everything really *was* good, surprisingly enough. Tigre knew every restaurant in town, every joint that amounted to anything at all in good old San Berdoo. Given the size of his family, he was probably related to all of the owners too. They certainly treated him like kin—and us along with him.

That afternoon, we had another meeting of our incipient group of investigators in my hotel suite.

Dastrie and I brought the others up-to-date on our discoveries and adventures, and then I opened the floor for discussion.

"*Señor*," Tigre interrupted.

I nodded at him to continue.

"You ax me about *Señor* Rowlings and what he do here in thees place?"

I nodded again.

"I talk to my cousin Goliat, and he say that the *señor*, he get very drunk and spend *muchos dólares*. He do thees more than one time. Once he take off hees, uh, hees dress."

"He ran around naked?" Dastrie commented. "How utterly divine! I'll never be able to look at Kenneth in quite the same way again."

"*Sí*," Tigre agreed, "*desnudo*."

"Did anyone try to help him?" I asked.

"*Señora* Rowlings and *Señor* Havens, they come here several times."

"When did the last incident occur?"

"Six week, maybe?"

"Thank you," I replied. "Anyone else?"

"Yeah," Laz O'Riley spoke up. "When Dr. Rowlings lived in New York he got himself in hock to the wrong people. He was beaten up at least once that I know about. I think Mr. Havens eventually bailed him out, but it wasn't long after that the Rowlings moved west. My nose tells me there's something else here, too. I just have a feeling there was more involved than money."

"Keep on it," I ordered.

I knew more about the situation than I let on, but I wanted to see what he could find out himself.

"Dr. Rowlings pawned a couple of rings two months ago," Nate added. "I didn't realize it at first because he did the dirty in Fontana, where I don't have as many sources. He apparently has a pattern of leaving stuff at places like that and then redeeming them a few weeks later."

"Did he recover these items as well?"

"Yes."

"See what else you can find out."

"Zinc," I added, turning to the "heavy," "I want you to put your ear to the ground and see if Rowlings has any connections with the local mob. I know they're not big time, but there's got to be something out here equivalent to our lot in New York."

"Yeah, boss," he responded. "It's all mixed up with the gov'ment out here."

"I figured as much," I said. "Some things just never change. See if our good doctor has a, uh, reputation with these guys. Does he borrow money from them, does he gamble with them, that sort of thing."

"How did The Phantom's Phantom know where we'd be this afternoon?" Dastrie wanted to know.

A great silence filled the room.

"Someone either told him or we were followed," I finally stated.

"But nobody knew where we were going," Dastrie pressed.

"Yes, but I informed Tigre of our destination when I met him in the lobby," I admitted. "That was stupid of me, I can see now, because there were several other individuals lounging in the area."

"And one of them reported back to someone else," Dastrie indicated.

"We all have to be more careful," I finally said. "Our very steps are being shadowed. However, we know now that there's someone in the hotel who has direct contact with our enemy."

"Or maybe he's here himself," she noted.

"Maybe he's here himself," I agreed.

Then I invited the group to dinner in the Palmatoria Room, where we ordered steaks all around, all except Dastrie, who did finally get her salad, with a little dressing on the side. We spent the meal surveying our fellow diners, wondering which of them was the enemy.

None of them volunteered an answer.

VIII.

"I KNOW WHAT YOU WANT!"

▲

And liberty plucks justice by the nose.
—William Shakespeare

▼

SAN BERNARDINO, CALIFORNIA
TUESDAY, 27 OCTOBER 1953

I was having breakfast with Dastrie Underwood in the Alta Dining Room when the notes were delivered. The envelopes contained officially printed invitations from the hotel, asking us to participate in the Halloween costume party scheduled for Saturday evening.

"Look on the back, Richard," my companion suddenly exclaimed.

I flipped over the card, and sure enough, there was a message from my nemesis again, written in a bold black flair: "I KNOW WHAT YOU WANT!"

"I've got one too," Dastrie stated, showing me hers.

"Then I guess that we'll both have to attend," I replied. "You have something suitable to wear?"

"I can throw a few things together," she indicated. "What about you?"

"Ah, I have just the thing," I said, smiling.

She looked at me with that sideways grin of hers that I found so attractive, and then laughed out loud.

"Of course!" she exclaimed, clapping her hands together. "Of course! How utterly divine!"

The waiter suddenly was hovering over us.

"You called, madam?" he inquired.

"Another coffee, Peleo."

She was still nibbling on her Melba toast when sheriff's deputy H. John Deutschendorf was escorted to our table by the *maître d'*. I motioned him to have a seat, and asked him if he wanted anything.

"Just some of that hot black brew, sir, if you please," he replied.

I nodded to Peleo, who soon returned with a third cup and saucer.

"You know what this is about?" I asked the cop.

63

"Yes, sir, Sheriff Jardine told me to cooperate with you. You wanted to know about the accident last week at San Bernardino and Alabama."

"You were one of the investigating officers on the scene, I believe," I continued.

"Actually, me and Deputy Starkey were the first two men to arrive."

"Who called in the initial report?" I wanted to know.

"It was an anonymous tip," came the reply. "The dispatcher received a message about 7:00 PM that a car had been struck by a train on San Bernardino Avenue."

"The engineer didn't make the call?"

"No, sir, he had no way of doing that. This particular line only uses written work orders. The drivers aren't issued radios like on the main track. In any case, the man wasn't thinking straight."

"What about the watchman in the packing house?"

"Well, sure, I guess it could have been him," Deutschendorf stated.

"Did you actually interview the night guard?" I pressed.

"I never saw him myself. My partner told me afterwards that he'd talked to him just briefly. He said the guy'd confirmed that he'd heard a big 'boom' about seven, but added that he was a boozer who'd obviously been sleeping on the job, and didn't know nothing else."

"What's your partner's name?"

"Richard—Dick—Starkey. He's supposed to see you later."

"Was there a car parked out back of the warehouse?"

"Don't know, sir," the deputy replied. "I didn't check behind the place initially, and afterwards, well, there were so many vehicles around that anybody could've been there."

"Very well, tell me what you know about the incident," I said.

He then gave us a rendition that was pretty much identical to what we'd already heard from the railroad dick.

Dastrie had one final question for the officer.

"Mr. Deutschendorf," she said, "do you have any doubt in your own mind that this *was* an accident?"

"No, ma'am, I don't," he replied. "I found a broken bottle of scotch in the front compartment of the vehicle, and there was an odor of alcohol on the dead man's clothes. My partner can confirm that. I think the man just drank too much and pulled to the side of the road to sleep it off, not realizing that he was straddling the railroad track. When the train came along, he woke up enough to try and get out, but was too befuddled to stagger to safety.

"It happens, folks, it happens a lot. I've witnessed all too many stunts like this in my day."

"What about the fact that Mr. Havens exited the right side of the car?" I asked.

"People do funny things sometimes, sir," came the reply, "particularly when their judgment's impaired. You'd be surprised. No, I saw nothing at the scene—and I've seen nothing since—that would lead me to any other conclusion than what I put in my report."

"Thank you, deputy," I stated, dismissing him with a wave of my hand.

His partner showed up a few minutes later.

"Did you see the night watchman?" I asked.

"Toriano Jackson?" the officer replied. "Yes sir, I rousted him out about eight o'clock by banging repeatedly on the back door. He was dead drunk, and all he could remember was a 'clap of thunder'—obviously the sound of the train wreck. He also heard 'loud voices' arguing outside sometime before that, but given his state of mind, I don't think you can rely too much on anything he said, or when it might have occurred."

He also didn't know whether there was another car parked in the lot behind the facility at the time he arrived.

"Frankly, sir, we were too busy trying to see if the victim was still breathing, even though he was badly cut up—and Jack was calming down the engineer, who was almost hysterical. And then the emergency vehicles arrived, and everything was just chaos. It took us half the night to clean up the mess. The railroad had to send a crane down the track."

And that's all he knew.

There was a message waiting for me when I got back to my room, so I dialed Laz O'Riley's number.

"I found the watchman," he said, when he picked up the receiver.

"Where?"

"He's holed up at a place called the Lazy Daze Ranch in Badger Canyon."

"Sounds pretty rural," I commented.

"Yeah, it's out north of town on the other side of the water train tracks, up near the base of the mountains. There's a dirt road from Kendall Drive that winds through the vineyards, passing by Badger Hill before entering the cut. You can't miss it!"

The other message was from Muriel, inviting Dastrie and me to dine at the Rowlings house in Redlands on Wednesday evening. After checking with Dastrie, I quickly phoned an acceptance.

I ordered the car for afternoon, but when I told Tigre our destination, he gave me a funny look and said, "You do not want to go there, *señor!*"

"Why not?" I asked.

He muttered something under his breath about "*Las majas desnu-das*," shaking his head all the while, and again repeated his warning, "You do not weesh to go there, *señor!*"

"Nonetheless," I stated, "that is where we *will* go, El Tigre!"

Dastrie giggled.

"I think we're about to embark upon another little adventure again, Richard," she said.

"Just what we need, eh?" I replied, settling into the back seat.

We drove down Waterman to Fortieth Street, and then across the railroad tracks at Electric Avenue, and thence to Kendall, another mile distant, and followed the road north. Off to the right was a small airstrip, but other than that, the landscape was just weeds that had been burnt crisp by the long, hot months of the summer sun, waiting for the right combination of wind and spark to start a conflagration.

"Doesn't it ever get green around here?" Dastrie wanted to know.

"In the winter it ees *verde*," our driver said, "when the rains, they come."

Then we turned off on a rough dirt road that headed east towards the mountain range looming above us. I could see a series of small canyons cut into the side of the hills.

"Why is it so straight along the base?" my companion inquired.

"*La falla de San Andreas*," Tigre said.

"What?"

"The San Andreas Fault," I repeated.

"Oh, of course!"

We skirted a double hill on the right, and then headed through a rising pasture towards a small cleft in the mountainside. Just as we entered the canyon, we slipped under an arched metal sign proclaiming "Lazy Daze: Free at Last!"

"That's strange," Dastrie commented.

There was a small stream running down the gulley to our right, which was partially filled with a grove of trees.

We came to the compound soon thereafter. Tigre let us out at the main door, and then parked the car in the adjoining dirt lot.

The interior of the place was dark, but we could make out a shirt-less, middle-aged man standing behind a counter to the right. I remember thinking that his bulging tummy wasn't exactly the most attractive call-ing card that I could remember—but to each his own.

"Hey there, welcome to Lazy Daze, folks," he intoned. "Don't recall having seen you two before."

"No, we're new in town," I said.

"Guests are always welcome," the attendant stated, humming to himself. "I'm Steve Georgiou. That'll be two bucks apiece, please."

I gave him a fiver, and he asked us to sign the register.

"You can change over there, Dick," he added, pointing to a couple of stalls on the other side of the room.

"Change?" Dastrie inquired.

"Oh yes, here's your change," Georgiou indicated.

He gave me a one-dollar bill and handed us each a packet.

"These are the keys to your lockers. There's also a list of the rules inside. Enjoy yourselves, folks. We're all about freedom here: freedom of spirit, freedom of movement, freedom of space. We even have a few bungalows you can rent if you decide to stay on awhile. If you have any questions, hey, please don't hesitate to ask. We're very informal here: first names only."

"Well, thanks, Steve," I said, smiling and looking around the mostly bare room. "What, uh, what exactly do we change into?"

The proprietor laughed out loud a couple of times.

"Hey, that's a good one, Dick! It really is. You're a real pair of cut-ups. I can see you're going to fit right in here."

Georgiou pointed to a sign plastered over the exit on the other side of the room: "NO CLOTHES BEYOND THIS POINT!" it proclaimed.

"You can change into whatever God gave you, Dick."

"Oh, my," Dastrie exclaimed, and then she started laughing too. "Well, *Dickie*, this should be interesting."

I was glad then for the darkened nature of the room, because my face, I'm sure, had turned beet red with embarrassment.

"We're, uh, looking for a friend of ours named Jackson," I finally managed to get out.

"Tory? He's in No. 6, right next door to the weak-minded guy who calls himself Emperor Norton II of the Inland Empire. Just bang on the door. If he's sobered up, he'll talk to you. We don't allow no booze in here. One of our rules, you know."

"Come on, *Dickie*, it's time for us to go meet the gang!" Dastrie exclaimed, dragging me over to the stalls that lined one side of the room.

I swear, getting undressed in that place was one of the hardest things that I've ever had to do in my life. I've faced down cold-blooded killers and utterly heartless gangsters, I've confronted a dozen men with guns blazing, and I've gone up against the worst of the worst—but all of that was easier than what I had to do then.

I slowly stripped away my clothes and my pretensions, carefully bundled them up, and locked them away in the small metal cabinet behind me. It was like storing away my soul.

"*Dickie!* I'm still waiting for you, dear," Dastrie warbled.

"Cut the 'Dickie' crap," I muttered, pushing open the chest-high door. I kept my eyes carefully averted from the charms that my companion so blissfully and unselfconsciously displayed. All we were allowed was a pair of sandals each to keep our feet from being burned.

Then we ventured out into the stark raving beams of the mirthful, merciless sun. Everywhere that I looked, every direction that I peered, was filled with rampant nakedness: old, young, fat, slim, saggy, firm, tall, short, every possible combination except black.

Off to the right and up against the canyon wall was a well-kept swimming pool, with a green slope creeping halfway up the hill above, topped with a grove of palm trees; to the left I could see the tennis courts and another line of well-maintained bushes; and right smack dab in front of us across the square was a row of small, one-room bungalows, flanked to either side by several large buildings.

People went out of their way to come over and welcome us new-comers, and I tried very, very hard to avoid staring at anything but their eyes and noses and mouths and…well, at nothing south of the border, so to speak. It was very hard.

"So nice to have you visit," they exclaimed, one and all, as if we were old friends of the family.

"Come on, dearie," Dastrie said, interlinking her arm with mine, "time to go to work."

Gad, I could feel the warm, sweaty flank of her hip rubbing and bumping against mine, and I almost lost it right there.

We sauntered slowly towards the bungalows, everything dangling out. I was having a great deal of difficulty maintaining control.

"I wonder if they have some suntan lotion?" my companion mused. "You could lather it on for me."

"Oh, sure," I remarked, "That would be a winning scenario."

"Lighten up, *Dickie!*" she chuckled. "Enjoy yourself. I certainly am."

She laughed out loud a second time. I think she really was getting a huge kick out of my evident befuddlement, which just made my situation worse, of course. I have never felt so completely out of my element.

Mercifully, however, we finally came to No. 6, where I rapped several times on the door.

"Yeah?" growled the voice from within.

"Tory?" Dastrie cooed. "Tory, is that you, baby?"

The door popped open right away, and the man inside ran his eyes up and down my companion's ripe body. He would have put them on stalks if he could.

"Do I *know* you?" he gasped, his attention constantly engaged by the moving scenery.

"Aren't you going to invite us in, Tory?" my companion warbled.

"Yeah, yeah, sure, come on in," he said, moving back out of the way. "Have a seat over there"—he motioned to a ragged wreck of a couch, and then pulled up a chair opposite us. "You want something cold to drink?"

"Tea, if you've got it," I said, and Dastrie agreed.

The man was back in an instant, handing us smudged glasses filled with ice and some fluid with dark specks swirling around inside.

"Instant's all I got," he mumbled. "What can I do for you?"

"That train wreck in front of the packing house," I stated. "You were there, Tory."

"Yeah, well, maybe I was and maybe I wasn't," Jackson replied. "What's it to you, anyway?"

Dastrie was trying very hard to keep all of her parts covered from his prying eyes—not very successfully, I might add. I could see his problem myself.

He was a gray-haired man in his fifties with a big gut and dirty toes. One thing about nudity: everything's right up front where you can see it. I wasn't that much younger myself, but I was sure as hell in far better shape.

"We're investigating the incident," Dastrie whispered, smiling. "You want to help us, don't you?"

"Sure, baby," he muttered, "if you're willing to help me in return."

"We'll help you keep your job," I responded, frowning at the man. "You were drunk that night."

"Hey, I get drunk lotsa nights. So what? Boss doesn't care, so long as I'm safely inside."

"Oh, really?" I retorted. "So he knows that he's paying you good money for boozing on the job and not keeping your eye on things."

"Uh…."

"I thought so. What did you see and hear that night?"

"Look, I told all this to the cops already," Jackson stated.

"Tell it to us all over again," I ordered. "We're not the cops."

"I came on duty around five as usual, made my first rounds, and then locked the place up. When I got bored, I opened my flask."

"What else?"

"There *ain't* nothin' else. Oh, I heard some people outside maybe an hour or two later—not sure of the time—they were yelling at each other, cursing really, I dunno what about exactly. I shouted at them to shut up, and they did. I just drank some more after that, and I was starting to really feel fine when I hear this screech and bang out front, like somebody put on the brakes and then hit something. Then I hear this guy yelling his head off and I tell *him* to shut up, see, only he doesn't hear me, so I called the cops and then went back to my flask. Later there was all this commotion outside, but I was heading down that slope by then and fell sound asleep, I think, until somebody started pounding on the door. They told me there'd been an accident, and that some old duffer had died."

"The people you heard arguing—where were they?"

"Uh, well, I think they were out back. I heard a car door slam too, and somebody started an engine and drove off, but I don't know the time."

"What were they saying, Tory?" Dastrie pressed.

"Things like 'idiot' and 'stupid' and 'fool' and stuff like that. But it was all pretty foggy by that point, and I wasn't really paying attention. I just wanted them to shut up, you know, so I yelled at them myself through the door, and then they did."

"Could you tell us anything else about them?"

"Like what? It was these two people, OK? They were yelling at each other. One was mad about something, and the other was mad right back again. I dunno who they were."

I knew we weren't going to get anything else out of the watchman, so I nodded towards the door, and we went back out into that unremitting glare again. I don't how the Californians can stand all of that sunshine all year 'round. Dastrie made a beeline straight towards the pool.

"What're you doing?" I yelled.

"It's hot out here," she tossed over her shoulder, and then arched that lovely back and ass towards the sky as she made a running dive into the cool blue waters.

"And it's just lovely in here!" she cooed from the refuge of the pool, turning over on her back and playing the mermaid.

I needed no further invitation, but jumped into the fray myself. The shock of the cold water made me gasp. It was late October, after all, and the natural rays of Old Man Sol were no longer sufficient to keep the artificial pond heated to body temperature—or anywhere near it!

Still, it was hot enough that I felt greatly refreshed by our few minutes of fame and fortune at the Lazy Daze Ranch.

"Hey, you all come back now!" Steve exhorted, as we finally exited the premises.

"Real soon," I mumbled, while Dastrie tried to control the smirk that threatened to drip from her lips.

She smoothed her ruined hairdo back into a bun, and fixed it with a pin from her purse.

"That'll do until we get back to the hotel," she stated.

Then she looked at me out of the corner of her eye.

"That wasn't so bad now, was it, *Dickie*?"

"Would you *please* stop calling me 'Dickie'," I begged. "I hate that name."

"You're right," she said. "It wasn't a 'dickie' at all, from what I could see."

It took me a second to "get" it. I suddenly turned bright red again. Then I couldn't help myself: I just started laughing, and so did Dastrie, her eyes sparkling. She had this perfect set of brilliant white teeth, good enough to eat you with.

"What ees so funny, *señor y señorita*?" Tigre wanted to know.

"Oh, nothing," I replied. "Nothing at all."

And then we both started on another round of guffaws.

It *was* a great day to be alive.

IX.

"I KNOW HOW YOU MOVE!"

▲

Gentlemen Prefer Blondes.
—Anita Loos novel

▼

SAN BERNARDINO, CALIFORNIA
WEDNESDAY, 28 OCTOBER 1953

I had every intention on Wednesday of conducting a meeting of our little group that afternoon, before heading over to the Redlands residence of Dr. and Mrs. Rowlings for "din-din," but the best-laid plans of Moses and his merry men sometimes go awry—and so did I, so did I.

First, however, Dastrie and I were determined on that bright sunny morning to essay the hotel's renowned mud baths. The mucky goo was created in several large concrete-lined pits located out back of the resort. These were fed by some of the hot springs for which the spa was named; indeed, the natural outpouring of the mineral water at different locations on the site was so prodigious—and emerged at such high temperatures—that it often had to be cooled before it could be touched by human skin. The 170° F liquid was the hottest natural outflow anywhere in North America.

The steaming, dark brown muck was trucked by hand carts to a series of small rooms in the hotel basement, and packed into each recessed basin. The bather would climb into the open tub, and his or her body would be engulfed until the stuff had almost reached the chin. It was like being wrapped in a soothing, sloshing blanket of slush. I felt like the Wizard of Ooze, and mentioned this to Dastrie, who occupied the "muddle" next to me.

"Ohhh!" she exclaimed, "that's terrible, Richard! You should be ashamed of yourself."

"No shame whatever," I replied, and indeed I hadn't.

I'd come to enjoy my lady's company so well that the thought of returning to my humdrum existence in the Big Apple no longer much appealed to me.

"I wish this would go on forever," I muttered, not even realizing that I'd spoken the words out loud.

72

"So do I," she agreed, looking at me and grinning in a way that I hadn't seen before.

She was one of those people whose face was just utterly illuminated by her smile: it transformed her and it transfixed me, and I thought that it was the loveliest thing that I'd ever seen in my life. I told her so.

"Why, thank you, my dear," she replied.

No false modesty here: it was one of the facets of her character that I particularly relished. I'd come to hate the standard socializing and BS-ing that typified so many of the interactions that I was used to among the powerful and financial elite of the East Coast.

"I don't see why this has to end," Dastrie continued. "You see, I know who you are, Richard."

That was a very strange thing for her to say under the circumstances, and I wondered for a moment if I *really* knew who Dastrie was, other than a vital, captivating, and utterly sexy witch.

I lay back and closed my eyes, making no further response, just allowing the hot muck slowly to embrace and caress my limbs. Every so often an attendant would appear to bring us towels, cold water, or whatever else we desired. But I just drifted lethargically away into Never-Never-Land.

It seemed to me then that I was being brought before the bar to account for my many crimes against humanity, for all of the times that I'd broken the law to bring justice to the city, for all of the bodies that I'd left rotting in the gutters of the Five Boroughs.

I was standing in the dock when the bailiff announced, "All rise! The Unified Court of Gehenna and Hades, Division DCLXVI, is now in session, the Honorable Alger X. Histamine presiding. The gods save this high and mighty court.

"Case No. 666, Your Honor: The Collected Shades vs. Richard Curtis Van Loan, who calls himself The Phantom."

"Read the charges," the judge intoned.

"That the defendant, on two thousand, six hundred, and twenty-seven separate occasions, did take the law into his own hands, thereby violating multiple federal, state, county, and city ordinances; and did act as judge, jury, and executioner, without giving those accused the benefit of a hearing, trial, or even a consideration beyond the open barrel of a gun; and that Richard Curtis Van Loan, the so-called Phantom Detective, did willfully murder John Q. Public and John Doe and several thousand of their compatriots, all on his own initiative and without the benefit of the law. This we do allege and charge, Your Honor."

"Is counsel for both sides ready?"

"Fra Torquemada, Assistant DA for the prosecution: ready, Your Honor."

"Grigory Rasputin, attorney for the defense. I'm also ready, Your Honor."

"Very well," the judge intoned, "let us proceed."

"Wait a minute!" I interjected. "I've not had a chance to talk with my lawyer."

"Father Torquemada?" Histamine asked.

"Irrelevant, Your Honor: in Down Under-World such consultation is not required by law."

"Sustained! Please continue."

"The crimes that have been alleged were in fact committed by the defendant," the prosecutor continued. "Therefore, the prisoner is guilty as charged and ought to be condemned forthwith. QED."

"Mr. Rasputin?" the judge said.

"Well, of *course* my client committed these acts of perfidy and perdition, but that's who he is, isn't it? He shouldn't be punished for doing what comes naturally. There's not a shade among us who could say differently. We're all guilty: that's why we're here!"

"Here! Here!" the onlookers chanted.

"Order in this court; I will have order in this court!"

The judge banged his gavel, an old yellow skull, repeatedly down on the podium. It went "knock, knock, knock."

When things quieted down, the prosecutor stepped forward once again. He was wearing a bright red cape.

"*¡Escila y Caribdis!*" Torquemada exclaimed. "That's not the point. He's guilty and must be punished! Just as we have all been punished, Your Honor."

He had a rough Spanish accent.

"Agreed!" Histamine stated.

"Guilty!" the audience shouted. "Guilty! Guilty!"

Then the judge looked gravely down at me.

"Richard Curtis Van Loan," he intoned, "you have been accused of some of the most heinous crimes ever recorded in these lands. Do you have anything to say before sentence is passed?"

"But, but, you didn't give me a chance to mount a defense!" I cried.

"We gave you the same chance you gave your victims," came the retort.

The judge put a black cloth over his head, hiding his face.

"It is the sad duty of this court to pass final judgment on the defendant. Richard Curtis Van Loan, you have been found guilty on all counts. I sentence you to...."

About that time, I felt someone grab my ankles, and I was suddenly yanked backward into the tub, my head abruptly slipping beneath the surface of the mud. I instinctively tried to breathe in, and starting choking as the muck clogged my mouth. My legs were being held well above the level of the basin, so that I couldn't get the leverage to wedge myself out again. I tried putting both of my arms over the lip of the bath, and managed to yank myself up for one quick cough and subsequent gasp of air before slipping back down into the ooze again.

I heard Dastrie scream my name—"Richard!"—while I was struggling to rise against my attacker. Then my left foot abruptly came free, and I was able to pop up and catch another quick breath. I glimpsed Dastrie fighting the man for control of my legs, screeching for help at the top of her lungs. Finally the assailant let go and bolted for the exit as the real attendants responded to my companion's calls for assistance.

Then she was pulling me out of the mire, both of us covered from head to toe with the brown stuff, and I was choking down huge breaths of fresh air. Dastrie was crying and laughing at one and the same time, her nearly bare body wrapped around mine, wiping the goo from my eyes and nose, and kissing me over and over again on my lips.

"I thought you were done for," she managed to gasp out.

"God help anyone who gets between me and thee," I said, and she kissed me on the lips once more.

Our assistants wrapped us in towels and fluffy white bathrobes and took us into the showers to get dowsed by cleansing sheets of almost scalding water. By the time I got back to my room, I was utterly exhausted, but before I did anything else, I phoned Muriel and the "boys" and canceled our plans for the rest of the day. We'd have our meeting of The Phantom Detective Agency on Thursday afternoon, and Muriel rescheduled the dinner for Friday night. I was hanging up the receiver when someone banged on the door.

I checked very carefully before opening the aperture wide. It was Dastrie, of course.

"I can't stay there by myself," she said, coming straight into my arms. "I don't want to be alone, Richard."

Then she saw the lines etched under my eyes, and was immediately concerned.

"You need to rest," she stated. "You were almost killed today."

"I think our enemy is escalating the stakes," I murmured, almost asleep on my feet. "We need some weapons. Phone Zinc for me, would you, please."

Then I sat down on the bed and let myself fall backwards. I was out before I hit the pillow. I vaguely felt Dastrie tucking me in and making a call, and then I knew no more. At some point a few hours later I realized that there was a warm, soft body snuggled up close to mine—and I smiled.

A little bit later I decided that I'd slept quite enough, thank you, and I turned over, put my arms around that wonderful warmth, and

75

gradually kissed my girl awake. It was then that I learned a great deal more about Dastrie Lee Underhill.

"Under the hill and through the woods," I chuckled.

"Oh, you're a wicked, wicked man, Richard!" she replied, moving one of her hands in a particularly intimate clutch.

"Then how about this?" I countered, and she squealed.

"Wicked!" she whispered, arching her body in a sudden spasm.

It was some time before we went down to brunch or dinner or whatever the hell it was.

We were seated at a table for two in one corner of the Palmatoria Room, right beneath a huge artificial candelabrum, the signature decoration of the main dining and dancing area of the hotel.

Dastrie lifted her napkin off the table, and then dropped it like it was burning. She couldn't say anything, but just pointed, her fingers trembling, her lip quavering.

I picked up the limp cloth and turned it over. Scrawled on the bottom in a bold black hand was a message writ just for her: "I KNOW HOW YOU MOVE!"

"He *knows*!" she whispered, staring daggers at the diners in the room. "He *knows*, Richard!"

I covered her hand in mine and squeezed it to calm her fears.

"He couldn't," I said. "It's just a coincidence."

"No, he *knows*, Richard! Why *me*?"

"He's here somewhere," I replied. "He's here and he's watching us, but he won't make his move until Saturday."

"How do you know?" she asked, her voice still shaking.

"The message he sent us yesterday was an invitation to the Halloween Ball. That's where everyone will be hiding behind their masks. That's where all the secrets will finally come out. That's where we'll meet him, Dastrie, one Phantom to another."

"You have to kill this man, Richard. He's crazy."

"I know."

I deliberately took several long breaths, and then motioned to a traveling waiter.

"I'm ready to order now," I stated.

Neither of us ate very much of our meal. I think the cook must have wondered where his cuisine had gone wrong. It wasn't the taste, it was the loss of appetite, but he had no way of knowing that, of course. We took our time and drank too much wine, and then we snuck back to my suite again, like two teenagers ready to make out in the park.

"Don't make me go back to my room," she begged.

I just smiled. How could I force her to leave? She was becoming an essential part of my life.

76

After we'd made love again, she finally drifted off to sleep, and I lay there wide awake, remembering full well why I'd never become seriously enmeshed with anyone during my years as a crime-fighter. I'd taken a vow of noninvolvement to avoid just this situation. Weaving such an intimate connection with another person made that individual a potential target for my enemies—and that in turn made my job that much more difficult. I became vulnerable because *she* was vulnerable.

But Dastrie Lee Underhill wasn't just any woman. She was younger than I, certainly as strong as I, and every bit as determined as I. Maybe I'd been wrong all those years. Maybe I should just have allowed the chips to fall where they may, and then let God or the Devil sort out all the rest. I'd lived too long alone and it had damaged me in some vital way, made me callous of basic feelings. I was a better killer because of it, to be sure, but was I a better man? I didn't think so. Maybe our new relationship offered me a way finally to redeem myself.

The phone rang. I sat up on the edge of the bed and picked it up. Dastrie bolted awake just next to me, holding onto my shoulder with one slim hand, while she leaned her head down close enough to hear.

"I KNOW HOW YOU MOVE!" came the whisper from the other side.

It was the voice of a ghost, slippery and smoky and slithery.

"Who the bloody hell *are* you?" I demanded. "What do you want from me?"

"Everything, Van Loan," the soft voice chanted. "I want the girl. I want the gold watch. I want everything else you possess. I want to see you ruined. I want to see you destroyed. I want to see you suffer."

"Why?"

"*Quid pro quo*, my little Phantomimist, *quid pro quo*. I do unto thee what thou hast done unto me."

Then Dastrie grabbed the instrument out of my hand, and before I could do anything to stop her, put her ruby lips together and whistled a shrill, high note that would have set the 8 AM shift going at the local railroad yard. It must have blasted his eardrums off. I heard a yelp of pain.

"You do anything to him, you bastard," she yelled into the phone, "and you'll have to deal with me next!"

She slammed the black receiver back down on its cradle.

"Well, that told him!" I noted.

"Damn right!" she stated, smiling slightly. "I'm not like most women, Richard."

"I'd noticed that, actually," I replied.

"Really? How?"

"Well," I said, "there's this"—"Oh!"—"and this"—"Ohhh!"—"and this"—"Oh, Richard!"

Sometime early the next morning, the light from the moon that was pouring into our room roused me from my slumber, and I slowly slipped out of bed and quietly padded in my bare feet over to the open window. I'd rented #620, a suite located at the top center of the complex, the same room that had once been occupied by Marilyn Monroe. Her latest star vehicle was *Gentlemen Prefer Blondes,* based on the Anita Loos novel of the same name, which had been released just this past June.

But Marilyn's hair color came out of a bottle and her name from an agent's inventiveness, and that kind of brittle, even shrill beauty carried no lure for me. Dastrie was the real thing, someone a man could rely on during both good times and bad. She had a strength of character that the Marilyn Monroes of this world couldn't begin to match.

I opened the curtains a bit wider. The view of the moonlit grounds sloping down into shadow was stunning, almost a fairyland of fantasy, all the bushes and flowers and plants caressed by lambent tongues of pale light, banishing any thought of evil.

I would do what I'd always done: I'd solve the twin mysteries confronting me and bring the criminals to justice. But it was also time for me to start living my life again. I'd waited far too long, I could now see. Thank God I'd had this vision while I still had the chance to change.

"Come back to bed, Richard!" the quiet, calming voice of reason chanted behind me.

"Yes, dearest," I replied.

X.

"I KNOW WHAT YOU SEE"

▲

Hannibal ad porteas (Hannibal's at the Gates).
—Old Roman warning

▼

SAN BERNARDINO, CALIFORNIA
THURSDAY, 29 OCTOBER 1953

I never did get back to sleep that morning. Instead, I did some se-rious thinking about Frank Havens and his life.

I'd never thought that Havens was a saint—none of us are, when it comes right down to it. A man who'd attained Frank's preeminent status in business, when he hadn't actually inherited any of his wealth, could only have achieved that position through exceptionally hard work, a single-minded attention to detail, and a willingness to do the dirty when necessary. To his credit, Havens had never claimed to be other than what he was.

That he also managed to salvage some internal moral ethics and sense of fair play was remarkable, and I admired him (and justifiably so) for his absence of rancor and his kindliness to those less fortunate than himself—including a war-damaged, shell-shocked young soldier named Richard Van Loan. Without Frank, I might have wound up as a perma-nent resident of the local mental facility.

But Havens had his rivals, in business as well as in his personal, social, and professional life. There'd been at least one occasion when those enemies had tried to frame Frank for extortion and bribery. The situation had been sufficiently unclear to everyone at the onset that real suspicion had fallen on the newspaper publisher. It had partially been a matter of interpreting the sequence of certain actions that Frank had taken to benefit a friend. In the end, it'd been clear to me—and I made certain that it was equally clear to the authorities—that Havens had operating completely above board at all times.

And there was something else too, just a hint of scandal that had attached itself to the publisher about a decade ago, in the midst of the World War against the Nazis. Kenneth Rowlings had then been serving as a Captain in the U.S. Army, as part of a team of doctors and nurses at

79

one of the major military convalescent hospitals on the East Coast. At the time I was, well, let's just say that I was fighting for Uncle Sam under the counter, so to speak. Although I'd officially been brought back into the service with the rank of bird Colonel, I was actually on detached duty with a super-secret organization based in Washington, DC.

Frank had taken the train down to the capital one steamy July afternoon and unexpectedly walked into my office, an office that wasn't supposed to exist. To say that I'd been surprised is an understatement. There should have been no way that Havens could have found me.

"I need your help, Van," Frank had said.

"Anything," I'd replied.

"Ken's gotten himself into an awkward position," he'd continued. "Some supplies have gone missing in the hospital where he works, and although he's not responsible for keeping inventory, he *is* the administrator of the department in question, and he's under pressure to provide an accounting to his superiors. I'm convinced that the materials were either lost or misplaced—or, at the worst, that one of the orderlies there pocketed a few bottles of penicillin to treat some relative."

"What can I do?" I'd countered. "This isn't my area."

"Ken feels he's being targeted, even though he's done nothing wrong, so he's put in for a transfer to another facility, *any* facility. But his request has been deep-sixed by the hospital administrator, who's expressed his personal dislike of Ken on more than one occasion. He seems to relish Ken's present discomfort. Could you pull a few strings and get him out of there? He doesn't really care where—even an overseas assignment would be preferable to the hell he's in now."

"I'll see what's possible," I'd promised.

I'd actually secured a billet for Rowlings at the Naval Recuperation Hospital that had just been established at the Hot Springs Hotel and Resort, the same facility where Dastrie and I were now staying. When the war had ended, Kenneth had remained in Southern California, eventually bringing his wife and family out west to join him.

Now I was beginning to wonder if that was the whole story about Dr. Kenneth Mortimer Rowlings, or whether something else had happened a decade ago.

When Dastrie began to stir, I made a long-distance call to DC. It took thirty minutes for the operator to ring me back. My old organization had morphed into another alphabet soup after the war, but most of the former operatives had become administrators in the new, greatly expanded official spy house of the US Government.

"What do you want, Richard?" my onetime colleague asked.

He certainly didn't appreciate hearing from me—or even the fact that he *could* hear from me so readily.

I explained what I needed.

"You know that we're not involved in domestic issues."

"This is old history," I noted. "All I want is some information from a file. You can easily obtain that record by just asking for it, and no one will ever question your authority."

"Very well. Richard. I owe you one. But this is the last time, old buddy."

"Agreed," I stated.

Just before Dastrie and I went down to lunch, my contact called back.

"I found something," he said. "I don't know what your man *really* did, but he sure as hell pissed off the hospital commandant, Col. Barry Pincus. Pincus did everything he could to cashier Rowlings, and it was all picayune stuff too, very obviously manufactured. It wouldn't have stuck, I don't think, but who the hell knows? It was lucky that someone higher up yanked the good doctor right out from underneath the colonel's jurisdiction."

"Yeah, well, lightning sometimes does strike twice."

"Sure it does, Richard. Sure. Like I said, this is it, old buddy. We're even now."

So what *had* Rowlings done in 1943? I was hoping that Laz O'Riley might have some better sources.

Luncheon was a few slices of *canard à l'orange* with a little *pâté* on the side, and some fresh apples and Roquefort cheese for dessert. Delicious!

Afterwards, we went for a dip in the huge swimming pool, a beautifully rendered facility with scalloped edges that had been designed by Esther Williams herself. It was kept heated all year 'round by the natural hot springs.

"I wonder if it's open at night," Dastrie said.

"Even if it isn't," I responded, "we might be able to sneak in."

"That'd be great fun!"—and with Dastrie involved, I'm sure that would have been true.

But we had our next meeting of The Phantom Detective Agency scheduled at two, so we couldn't linger overlong, alas.

One by one our "boys" filed into the room. Nate Zohn was the first to speak up.

"The Rowlings are in hock up to their proverbial chins," he stated. "Their house has been mortgaged twice, and there's an additional mortgage on the downtown medical office. This is strange, because Dr. Rowlings made a record amount of money last year.

"What's even stranger is that some of those earnings were unreported to the IRS. I don't know where they came from—certainly not from his gambling, where he seems to have been the quintessential loser, although again, not so obviously or to such an extent that it should have put him into this kind of financial difficulty."

"What about Havens's will?" I asked.

"The country estate goes to his widow. The stocks and bonds are divided equally between the widow and Mrs. Rowlings. The rest is complicated, and it would take months, I suspect, to sort it all out. Again, the two parties tend to benefit equally from whatever else is out there, except for the local business, which goes solely to the wife."

"What are we talking about overall?"

"I honestly have no idea: in the millions, certainly, although taxes might eat up some of it. All of the rest of the estate is buried beneath the interlocking layers of a series of shell corporations. It looks to me as if Havens had a controlling interest, one way or the other, in each of these businesses, but I'm really not sure."

"But both parties would inherit a substantial estate."

"Essentially, yes."

"Thank you," I acknowledged. "Mr. O'Riley."

"Well, sir," the Irishman said, "Dr. Rowlings came west because he was having difficulties getting along with the administrator of the Army hospital where he was stationed on Long Island. The official record was mucked around with, I suspect by Col. Pincus. He tried to get Rowlings removed over petty discrepancies in the storage of drugs in one of the supply rooms. It was obviously a put-up job.

"It took me brother Paddy several days and several hundred dollars to uncover the real story. Dr. Rowlings liked the young nurses. He liked them a whole lot. He got one of them knocked up. She agreed to let him take care of the situation in exchange for a thousand bucks worth of silence, but she died of bleeding the next day. Her body was found off base, and the death could never be tied officially to Rowlings, although Col. Pincus certainly suspected him. The only one who knew for sure, the girl's roommate, had acted as a nurse for the procedure; she took the money her friend would have had and kept her mouth shut. If she'd said anything, she would have been charged as an accomplice.

"Pincus did his best to persecute Rowlings, but somehow the man got reassigned to another hospital—and that was that."

I didn't tell them that *I'd* been the one who'd been set up. For one thing, I doubted that Frank had known the whole story. He never would have condoned that kind of activity—never!

"What about now?" Dastrie interjected.

"What do you mean?" Laz replied.

"Well, Mr. Zohn has just told us that Dr. Rowlings is making income that isn't being reported to the government. Where's it coming from? Could he have reverted back to his old tricks?"

"I can certainly find out," the P.I. indicated, grinning his crooked smile.

"Tigre, tell me about gambling in the Inland Empire."

"Ah, *señor*, eet ees right here in thees place!"

"You mean, in the Hot Springs Hotel?" Dastrie inquired.

"*Sí, señorita*," the driver said. "There are the rooms behind the rooms, many, many rooms that no one sees, except that they pay the price: rooms with beeg wheels that have leetle balls going around and around in them, rooms with the dice and the cards."

"But how do they get away with it? It's 1953, for God's sake."

"*Los policías*, they look the other way," Tigre responded, "for *muchos dólares*. But eet does not happen *mucho* anymore. Just when *los gordos* are here."

"The high rollers," I commented.

"*Sí, señor.*"

"And Dr. Rowlings is one of them."

"Sometimes, *señor*, or so my cousin Goliat say. They play *el póker.*"

"Of course," Dastrie said. "And the stakes are often very high."

"As you say, *señorita.*"

"Thank you, Tigre," I stated. "Zinc."

"Yeah, boss. I did like you said and nosed around the joints this week. Some of the 'tenders knew the Doc. Word on the street is he needs the dough real bad. They say he's got to put up real soon like, or he'll have to pay the bad boys the hard way."

"How much?" I asked.

"Ten, twenty big ones maybe."

"You got any names?"

Zinc shrank within himself and glanced around the room.

"Shouldn't talk about this stuff like this, boss. The walls, they've got ears, ya know."

"Still," I said.

He grunted a few times, and then slogged down half a beer.

"Uhh, Zed Lepplin's one. Maybe Bosco Fyffe. Heike the Whore down on 'D' Street was mentioned by somebody. It's all just rumbles, boss."

"Thanks, Zinc," I responded. "And now Dastrie."

"Regarding our other problem, this is what happened to us earlier this week"—she related our various adventures to the rest of the group—"The Sheriff's Department was unable to locate our assailant, but we have to assume that he's still present here in the hotel.

"I've also been on the phone with Liz Bordone back in New York. The murder of Count Bâtonrompe has been traced to Indochinese terrorists—he had business and political interests in that part of the

83

world—and Roscoe's untimely death was a simple mugging—the wrong place at the wrong time. The LAPD has been investigating the murder of Miss Guest, the woman who was sitting next to Richard on his flight west. They've recently interviewed the ex-husband, who was paying her a rather significant amount of alimony and had recently suffered several business reversals. There's been no progress with the slaying of Father Levine."

"Dastrie and I are having dinner with the Rowlings family tomorrow evening," I stated, "and I intend to press both of them with some of the findings you folks have discovered. Good work, everyone.

"I want all of you present here for the Halloween Ball on Saturday night. Bring a costume, something unique that we can use to identify each of you. I expect to confront The Phantom's Phantom there, and I'm going to need you as backup. Zinc will provide you with the appropriate weapons."

"What about the permits?" Dastrie asked.

"Zinc will have those as well"—I looked at him and he nodded.

"Keep sharp, everyone. Any of you could be attacked between now and then, if the killer identifies you as working with us. Laz, find me some confirmation quickly about the doctor's current involvement with a possible abortion racket.

"Thanks, folks."

Zinc lingered behind to give me and Dastrie our guns—mine a gleaming black Lugar and Dastrie's a pocketbook .22. Both would suffice. I expressed my gratitude to the man.

He just grunted as he exited the room.

Laz O'Riley phoned us an hour later.

"Got ya a name and an address," he indicated. "Roberta Anderson, 1564 Perris Hill Road, San Bernardino. She's renting the upstairs apartment. She was one of Dr. Rowlings's patients. She'll talk to you for a 'c' note."

Then he hung up.

Something was bothering me. Something just didn't add up.

I asked Dastrie to call Tigre and have the car brought around immediately, while I phoned the hotel desk. I wanted to send a telegram to a friend of mine, one of the last officers that I still knew in the NYPD. Most had retired long since, but Frank Castelluccio was a desk sergeant in the Two-Two Precinct. He owed me one big-time from the old days, when I'd saved his sister from the proverbial fate worse than death, and I knew he'd come through with an answer to my simple request. Given the difference in time zones, though, I probably wouldn't hear back from him until Friday.

In the meantime, Dastrie and I had another road trip to make.

The main entrance to the Hot Springs Hotel was located at the rear of the building, where the long, winding drive finally ended in a circle of worn asphalt. The entrance road was "long and winding," I was informed by Tigre, because whenever high-stakes gamblers were present, they hotel would post a flunky in one of the upstairs front rooms, just to keep an eye on the distant gate in case the cops showed up for one of their rare raids on the facility. They never found anything, of course.

We were soon headed down Waterman Avenue again. When we reached the hospital, Tigre turned onto Twenty-First Street, driving past the park on the left, and then following Perris Hill Park Road to Pacific. Two blocks left on Pacific brought us to Perris *Hill* Road, a completely different street from the other. I found this very confusing.

"Ees also a Park Road, *señor*," our driver commented, shrugging his shoulders at the inanity of the city planners.

He pulled up in front of an old, two-story building that looked like a farmhouse. It had a wooden stairwell stapled to the right-hand side of the structure, and we tramped up the stairs to the top, and then up another flight inside, knocking on the apartment door to our right.

"Yes," came the faint reply.

"We're here to see Roberta Anderson," I stated.

"Just a moment, please."

It was actually close to five minutes before she cracked the door.

"Mr. Van Loan?" she asked.

She had a voice like Minnie Mouse, squeaky clean.

"And Miss Underhill," I said.

"P-please come in."

She must have been all of twenty years old, with dark hair and glasses and lines already etching the corners of her eyes. She'd seen way too much of life, this girl, and she already knew that it wasn't going to get any better.

"I can talk with you for half an hour," she added, "before I have to go to work."

She was a clerk, she said, down at the family grocers at the corner of Perris Hill and Baseline.

I took the hundred-dollar bill out of my wallet and put it on the nearby bureau. Her eyes followed my hand like a serpent tracking its prey. It was far more than she earned in a paycheck.

There was just one chair, so Dastrie and I both sat on the end of the carefully made-up bed.

"I understand you were a patient of Dr. Rowlings," my companion began.

"No," the girl responded.

"But we were told…."

"When I, uh, got into t-trouble," she indicated, "m-my boyfriend decided he didn't w-want to marry me. I c-couldn't tell my p-parents. My father would have b-beaten me. S-so I asked around, and Jenny, well, she s-said that there was this man who could take c-care of it for me. S-so I took the bus over to Redlands, and waited for hours and hours in a dingy office, until this man showed up about dinnertime. He put me on a table in back, and d-did things to me. He s-said it was s-still p-possible, but he would have to do it s-soon.

"I asked h-how much, and he s-said two-fifty. I didn't have no more than fifty bucks to my name, and I t-told him s-so. He s-said '*no problemo*,' I c-could work it off. I s-said I already had a job, but he j-just laughed and laughed. He s-said I could work for M-Madame Heike for three months, and it would all be p-paid.

"S-so what else c-could I do? It w-was awful."

She hung her head, her dull bangs hanging to either side of her face, tears dripping down her cheeks. I felt immense sorrow for this poor creature that'd been trapped by ignorance and circumstance. Her life was ruined, or at least that's how she perceived it; and I determined to do something at a later date to help get her back on her feet.

"Let's return to Dr. Rowlings. You said he had a reputation of being able to provide this service," Dastrie pressed.

"S-some of my friends from high school, p-particularly Jenny, knew how to reach him. They d-didn't know his name, not up front. You had to first contact this man who ran the laundry s-service for the c-city of S-san Bernardino, and he'd make the d-date and tell you where to go."

"Then how do you know it was Rowlings?"

"When I w-was, when…"—she started crying quietly to herself, and couldn't say anything for a few minutes.

Dastrie, bless her soul, went over and put her arms around the girl, giving her what comfort she could. Finally Roberta was able to continue.

"At Madame Heike's p-place," she stated, "they had all s-sorts of c-customers. One day the d-doctor, he just shows up, and he goes off with D-duley. He liked the Negro girls. Things were s-slack then, and s-so the Madame, she put me to c-cleaning and dusting and the like, and I s-snuck upstairs where they were, you know, and I found where he'd s-set aside his coat, and there was a card inside that s-said who he was."

"You've been very helpful," I said. "No one will ever know that you've talked to us."

"*He* knows," she replied, wiggling her bangs back and forth.

"Who?" Dastrie inquired. "*Who* knows?"

"That Lazarus man. He was one of *them*. He paid Madame Heike to do things to me. I think he knows the doctor. He knows everyone! He *knows*."

86

The final words were no more than a whisper.

"Look at me!" I ordered, and the girl swiveled her eyes front and center.

"I won't let anyone touch you again," I stated. "I'll give you a real job and a real salary."

"But I d-don't know how to d-do anything," Roberta whined.

"If you need training, I'll pay for it," I promised. "Forget about the doctor. Forget about Madame Heike."

"I c-can't," she stuttered. "I'll never f-forget, s-sir. Never!"

And she started crying again.

We left a few moments later.

"It's the little people that always get hurt," I muttered to Dastrie, as we trod down those shoddy stairs.

"She's damaged for life," Dastrie agreed, "but we still have to help. I think we can salvage something worthwhile there—and she'll be devoted to you for the rest of her life."

"But what about Laz?" I stated, as we headed towards the car.

"If he does know Dr. Rowlings personally and hasn't told us, I wonder what else we don't know about his connections."

"Indeed," I said. "I think we should pay a visit to the good Madame and see what we can see."

"I'm game," my companion replied.

So I asked Tigre to take us there.

"You sure, *señor*?"

I said "*Sí.*"

South "D" Street had long been known as the place to go for certain kinds of entertainment in the Inland Empire. It was one long string of strip joints, sleazy beer halls, boxing studios, tattoo parlors, pawn shops, and houses of ill repute. The latter had diminished somewhat in numbers and splendor since their heyday during the recent war. In 1941 the local airbase had been constructed southwest of town, and had provided an unending number of green servicemen eager to do their duty for God, country, and the propagation of the species.

Of the establishments that still remained, Madame Heike's represented the apex of bad taste and wild living. Located in an old, three-story mansion south of the downtown area, the building looked entirely respectable in the light of the late afternoon sun. There was even a black wrought iron fence surrounding the place.

We strode right up to the front door, and used the brass knocker, which was shaped like one.

A man in a flannel shirt opened the door.

"Sorry, sir," he intoned, "we don't start till sunset."

"I'm not here for the service," I replied. "We want to see Madame Heike."

Before he could ask, I handed him my card.

"Very good, sir. I'll see if the Madame is receiving."

A few minutes later, he motioned us inside.

"Her office is located down the corridor to the left," he indicated.

There were no signs of the "employees," just a few cleaning ladies polishing the furniture. The *décor* was 1940s gauche, the walls being filled with paintings of an indiscrete nature, and the furniture being way too loud and ornate. The ruby carpet must have been an inch thick.

"Gad," Dastrie whispered, "you could fall into this place and never come out again."

"I think that's the general idea," I replied.

We came to a plain, unmarked door at the end of the hall and knocked loudly.

"Come in," came the order.

I don't know what I was expecting, but it certainly wasn't this. Heike was a little woman of about fifty, slim and short and beautifully coiffed. She wore an undecorated business dress, very simple, and one plain gold band adorned the index finger of her left hand.

"What can I do for you?" she asked.

I introduced Dastrie and then got right to it.

"I understand you know Dr. Rowlings," I stated.

"I know a great many people in this area," she responded. "It's my business. Dr. Rowlings regularly checks my employees to make certain that they're, uh, healthy."

"What other services does he provide?" I pressed.

"That's all he's contracted for," Heike indicated. "Whatever else he does medically is *his* business, sir, not mine. I believe his office is located in Redlands, but I've never been there myself. We don't travel in the same circles."

"I understand that you also know the detective, Laz O'Riley."

"The name does sound familiar to me," the woman noted, "but so many people come and go these days that I can't really keep track of them all. We're providing a service here, and a number of folks seem to like what we have to offer."

"But it's technically an illegal business, isn't it?" I said. "You could be shut down at any time."

"You could get hit by a car while walking down the street," the Madame observed. "Life is short and cruel, and we do what we can to survive—and I can see quite plainly that you've survived somewhat better than *moi*. Nothing is forever, though."

"Does Mr. O'Riley work for you on occasion?"

"Not in any formal sense," came the reply. "You must understand, Mr., uh, Van Loan, that many of my clients truly enjoy what I have to offer them, and they in turn have sometimes been willing to help me out. Mr. O'Riley is just another one of our satisfied customers, and when our customers are happy, well, sir, I'm happy too."

"Just one big happy family, eh?" I offered.

"As you say, Mr. Van Loan. We're all happy here."

I could see that we weren't going to get anywhere else with this slippery character. She'd been greasing the palms of the local politicos for far too long to allow herself to become entrapped by the likes of me, who had no official standing whatever.

I thanked her for her time.

As we were exiting the door, she piped up: "Oh, if your friend there is ever looking for a job, I might be able to help her, just like I helped Bertie. She's a little thin for my tastes, but I have several clients who like that sort of thing."

I thought Dastrie was going to exude claws and tear the woman to pieces right then and there.

"You damnable bitch," my companion growled. "You use people up and throw them away. You destroy the lives of the girls you employ, and then you harvest a brand new crop. I despise you."

Then she reared back and spat right across the room, a perfect hit. Heike carefully pulled out a handkerchief and wiped the moisture dripping from her nose.

"You're probably right," the Madame replied. "You're too old for this kind of work, too old and too bitter. Nobody would want you."

She looked past Dastrie to me.

"As for you sir, I KNOW WHAT YOU SEE!"

Then she grinned, an evil little smile of twisted triumph and trumpery.

I grabbed my girl and manhandled her into the corridor.

"It's not worth sinking to her level," I hissed into Dastrie's ear.

"But I'd sure like to," she whispered, and then ran ahead of me, right out the door and down the steps and out to the car.

She didn't say a word all the back to the hotel.

When we finally reached my room, she turned to me and said: "I hate everything that woman represents: the exploitation, the condescension, the despite, the casual abuse of girls who can't fight back, the corruption of local government, even the cynical traffic of the johns—even that. When they finally shut her down—and they will—she'll retire to the beach somewhere on her ill-gotten earnings, and live another twenty or thirty years sipping gin under an umbrella. She ought to be strung up on the nearest tree."

"Gee," I said, "I sure don't want to get on *your* bad side."

But she wouldn't smile back at me.

"It's not funny, Richard. It's mean and dirty and utterly, completely sordid. You saw what it did to Roberta Anderson, after just three months. Imagine working under those conditions for ten years—or longer!"

I had to agree, of course. She was absolutely right, as she usually was, and I was a damned fool if I didn't listen to her. But instead I just wrapped her in my arms and held her close until her anger began to fade, and then suggested that we go down to dinner.

After all, tomorrow was another day.

XI.

"I KNOW WHEN YOU DIE!"

▲

Hail, Cæsar! We who are about to die salute you!
—Roman gladiator saying

▼

REDLANDS, CALIFORNIA
FRIDAY, 30 OCTOBER 1953

I was munching on a scone at breakfast when the telegram from Sgt. Castelluccio was delivered. I signed for the message, tipped the bellboy a quarter dollar, and sliced the yellow envelope open with the bread knife. I scanned the contents and then passed the missive to Dastrie, who was sitting just across from me.

She looked up at after reading the note.

"You were expecting this, weren't you?" she stated.

"Let's just say I had a notion," I commented, "one that happened to pan out this time. There were too many coincidences to overlook. The answer had to rest somewhere in the past—*my* past, not Frank's or anyone else's."

"So what do we do?" she wanted to know.

"We do exactly what we'd intended to do anyway," I said. "We take a trip to the ball tomorrow night, where everyone and everything will finally be unmasked, where the pretensions and subterfuge will finally be stripped away."

"But won't *he* be there?"

"Oh, yes, I'm counting on it," I noted. "This has to end, Dastrie, or we'll be tormented by The Phantom's Phantom for years to come. He won't stop until he's forced to."

"And justice will be done?"

I put my bread down on the table and sighed.

"I'm not sure anymore whether justice is ever accomplished at the hands of man. We're too fallible, all of us. I've spent twenty years of my life trying to redress the balance, just a little, and I still don't know whether I've succeeded or failed. *He* would certainly have an opinion on that topic."

"Yes, and he'd be wrong too," my companion stated. "You took action when others couldn't, Richard. You did what had to be done during a time when the official institutions were almost wholly corrupted by the very elements that they were purporting to regulate. Somebody had to do what was necessary."

"But was it right?" I countered. "How many people, Dastrie? How many innocents got hurt in the process? How many of the public, the onlookers, the bystanders, even the relatives of the crooks? How many? That's what haunts me in the middle of the night. I see their faces crying out to me. So many times in the past I just pulled the trigger without ever thinking through the consequences. I was *right*, you see, and I knew it. I was the active agent of God's vengeance, to be wreaked and rained incessantly upon the criminous classes of North America. I was the lightning bolt that would purge the land of all its venom.

"And yet, look around our cities today. Are they any safer? Are they any cleaner? It's like the old Greek legend of the many-headed hydra: for each head you cut off, another ten grow in its place."

She reached over and placed her warm hand over mine.

"The battle never stops," she said. "The war is an eternal one, my dear. You're one of the soldiers that's taken up the lance and sword. You can't put them down now."

I smiled.

"No, I can't," I agreed, "anymore than the zebra can change its stripes. The alternating bands of black and white are just what he is. They're what I am too, I think."

"The difference, Richard, is that you have friends who can help you now. You're stronger because of us. You have to let go enough to see that reality. You have to build an organization that can attack the monster from many different sides and slice off *all* the heads at once."

"Is that really possible?" I wondered.

"I think it is," she countered. "At the least, it's a worthy goal. We'll do it together, my dear. I can wield a pretty good blade myself when I put my mind to it."

"I believe you could," I replied.

Just then the bellhop returned.

"There's a phone call for you at the main desk, sir," he said.

When I reached the lobby, I heard Cyndi's voice at the other end of the connection.

"I need to see you today at the ranch, if that's possible," she indicated.

"Afternoon OK?" I asked.

When she assured me that it was, I told her that we'd be there about one.

"I wonder what she wants," Dastrie mused.

I had no idea, but it was time in any event to bring Mrs. Havens up-to-date on the most recent developments in the case.

Tigre was waiting for us at noon at the hotel entrance. We brought along a couple of apples to munch on.

I was really enjoying the balmy climate and the clear air of Southern California. I could see that this area would be the next logical development of the huge metropolis that was being created by the expansion of Los Angeles out into the suburbs. The land here was very cheap now, but it wouldn't stay that way. A few judicious investments during the next few years would pay dividends for decades to come, and would be more than sufficient to establish The Phantom Detective Agency as a going concern into the indefinite future.

I outlined my plans to Dastrie, and she heartily agreed.

"You should buy a place here to serve as your western headquarters," she indicated. "You could spend half a year in New York and the rest in California."

"I thought that I'd make *you* the director of the organization," I stated.

"What!"

I could tell that she was completely nonplussed by the idea.

"You're young and dynamic and full of ideas," I indicated, "and you'd provide the continuity necessary to get the thing established and keep it going."

"But w-what about you?" Dastrie sputtered.

"I'd still be there," I indicated, "but I prefer to stand quietly in the background, as I've done throughout my career. I don't want to be a source of public comment. I find the spotlight of publicity excruciating, if you want to know the truth. You'd do a far better job at that than I could. You have an outgoing personality, and I don't. I suffer fools lightly, and that comes across to many people. Besides, I'm better at things like finance and actual crime-fighting than running an agency.

"All I ask is that you think about it."

She assured me that she would, and we rode along in silence most of the rest of the way. The hills were a dirty ochre color, covered with layers of dead or dying vegetation.

"It wouldn't take much to set this all ablaze," I noted.

"The wind, eet ees called *la Santana*," Tigre commented from the front seat. "When eet blows, and the torch, she ees lit, La California becomes *la tierra del fuego*."

"'The land of fire'," I translated.

By then we were approaching the entrance to Twin Pines Rancho, and it seemed to me suddenly a refuge from all the cares of the world, a place to which a man like me could retreat and rediscover his soul again. I breathed the dry, clean air very deeply into my lungs.

"It's beautiful, isn't it?" my companion commented.

"Indeed so," I agreed.

Cyndi was waiting for us at the front door.

"Come out back," she ordered. "We can sit there and enjoy the afternoon sun."

She'd already put out several iced teas for us, together with some homemade chocolate chip cookies.

"Where are the children?" Dastrie inquired.

"At school, of course. They have to take the bus into town. Actually, that's one of the reasons I wanted to talk to you, Van.

"I've decided to sell this place and move into Redlands. I'm going to try to keep the newspaper going, and it would be a lot more convenient for both me and the kids if we lived closer to town. I like the community and I think we'll do very well there. I'd be happy, though, if you'd consider taking the ranch off my hands—and I think Frank would approve, if he were here."

Now it was my turn to be surprised. I sat there sipping my tea in silence for a few minutes, watching a hawk circling over the ridge on the other side of the creek. The rise marked the far boundary of the property.

"A man could get used to this," I finally said. "Yes, Cyndi, I'll do it. Name your price and I'll have the papers drawn up next week. But only if Dastrie agrees to share the place with me."

"Of course I will," my companion replied. "I thought that was decided some time ago."

"I'm a little slow about these things," I indicated, chuckling. "I'm just beginning to figure it out."

"Congratulations!" Cyndi exclaimed. "I think you two are a great match. When's the date?"

"I haven't even made the tender yet," I stated.

"And I'm not sure that I'd accept anyway," Dastrie said. "I like our relationship just the way it is."

"Well, however it works out," Frank's widow continued, "I think you'll be good for each other. I can see the difference in Van already.

"But that's not the only reason I asked you here. I was going through Frank's things, deciding what to keep and what to give away, and I came across this."

She handed me an envelope marked "Frank Havens" in a bold, black hand. Inside was one of the three-by-five-inch white cards from The Phantom's Phantom:

"I KNOW WHEN YOU DIE!" it said.

"It was stuck inside this," she added, handing me a small ledger book. "I've never seen it before."

I flipped open the volume and quickly scanned the accounts.

"Frank was paying out money regularly to all kinds of people," Cyndi said. "I don't know who any of them are and I don't really want to know. I don't understand what was happening here, Van. I totaled up the amount for this year, and it came to $33,000. What was he doing that required that kind of expenditure? Frank was a very conservative businessman, and although he bet on the horses occasionally, it was always for fun: he didn't have a gambling problem. There isn't any reason for this."

"What do you really know about Dr. Rowlings?" I posed.

"Do you think he's involved?"

"I think Frank was trying to save his daughter from embarrassment. I think he was attempting to do the right thing here. He would have done anything for Muriel, just as he would have for you. These are probably Kenneth's debts."

"But how? And why?" Cyndi asked.

"He liked to gamble," I replied. "It's a sickness in some people. They can't seem to help themselves. I've seen it all before."

"Frank's estate is worth millions," she indicated. "I don't care about this chicken feed, Van. But it's got to stop, for the sake of their children, if nothing else. Promise me that you'll make it stop."

"I promise," I said, although God knows how I was going to do that. "We're having dinner there tonight. I'll talk to them then."

"Do you know yet what happened to Frank?"

"I have no idea," I lied.

"Please tell me when you can," she requested. "I've decided to scatter Frank's ashes here on Sunday. I'd really like to have you both present then."

I'd planned to fly back to New York that day, but I could easily postpone my trip.

"Of course," I responded.

The table under the patio suddenly started rattling.

"Earthquake!" Cyndi exclaimed.

It didn't last very long, but the shaking was certainly enough to unsettle someone who'd never experienced one before. When the ground itself wasn't safe any more, could mortal men fare much better?

On our way back to the hotel, Dastrie asked: "What are you going to say tonight?"

"I'm not sure yet," I said. "Tigre, I want you to linger in the kitchen and be prepared for anything."

"*Sí, señor.*"

When we returned to the resort, I phoned Lizzie back in the Big Apple, and had her postpone my travel indefinitely.

"I'm still not finished here," I noted.

"Just let me know, boss," my secretary responded.

Later that afternoon we went for a swim in Miss Williams's sparkling pool, figuring that The Phantom's Phantom wouldn't try anything in such a crowded venue. I mused again upon the information we'd received that morning, and wondered at the perfidy of people. Why now, after so many years? What had happened to create such hostility in the face of kindness?

I sat in the shallow end and allowed the waves generated by the bathers to wash over me, to cleanse my spirit of the blackness that lurked deep within my soul. I had to find some way of dispensing with this omnipresent anger and frustration if I was going to make something of my second life. Dastrie cuddled up next to me, the ugly bathing cap looking fetching on her when it seemed pretty gauche on everyone else. *She* was the answer, I thought, she was the balm of Gilead that would soothe the savage beast. I put my arm around her alabaster shoulders and held her close—and I smiled. She was just enough to make a difference for me. And as long as she'd have me, I'd never let her go.

"Penny for your thoughts," she said.

"Life is very good," I replied. "I don't think it's ever looked better."

"Even with the little challenges we have to face tonight and tomorrow?"

"Even so," I stated. "We'll face them together."

She reached up and took my hand in hers. She didn't have to say anything else. She just squeezed her fingers slightly, and I knew. It was sufficient for any man.

Then we went back to our respective rooms to change and get cleaned up for our command performance that evening.

Dr. and Mrs. Rowlings lived on Smiley Heights in Redlands, the apex of high society. We drove all the way up Waterman Avenue to the terminus of that road at Barton, where the cemetery was, and then took Barton south to Redlands, turning west on Terracina to reach the hills. The street wound in and out of undeveloped areas filled with citrus groves, interspersed with the fancy new homes that would gradually supplant them all, until it reached the Heights proper.

The wealthiest citizens of the region had relocated there from the old Victorian mansions that were scattered near the city center, placing themselves out of reach of the *hoi polloi*—except for the servants, of course. They looked down upon the rest of the town like the nabobs of old India, disdaining any concourse with the lesser creatures who occupied the lowlands.

Tigre left us at the base of the rise that climbed up to the front door, and then pulled the car around the block to the large driveway in the rear.

Dastrie rang the bell hanging under the bronze sign that proclaimed the place as belonging to "Dr. and Mrs. Kenneth M. Rowlings, MD," and the door was promptly answered by a Negro servant dressed in a black coat, white bow tie, and twin tails. I suspected that he'd been hired just for the occasion, along with the other workers who were catering the meal.

We were escorted into the living room, where the good doctor and his wife were waiting for us. Muriel offered us a drink, but I declined, wanting to keep my wits about me.

Soon we were ushered into the elaborate dining room, where the old oak table was lined with a five-pronged glittering candelabrum and several elaborate bouquets of greenhouse flowers. Since there were just the four of us, we occupied the points of the compass, my companion sitting across from me, with Muriel to my right and Kenneth to my left.

The first course was oxtail soup, a bit too salty for my taste, although the addition of garlic and onions redeemed the mix somewhat. This was followed by a dollop of sherbet served on a slice of orange to cleanse the pallet. The main course was rack of lamb, tender but a little greasy, with fresh green beans and a roasted garlic on the side, and scalloped potatoes. Dessert was a salad served with an unusual vinaigrette dressing, perhaps the best dish of the night, with a mix of fresh greens (including spinach and watercress), olives, goat cheese, slices of something sweet but crunchy called *jícama* (which I'd never encountered before), all sprinkled with a light, airy brew of vinegar, extra virgin olive oil, basil, and other herbs and spices. Outstanding!

When the servers had removed the final dish, we retired once more to the living room, where the Rowlings occupied what were obviously their favorite overstuffed chairs, the two visitors being relegated to the plush, red-and-green spotted sofa.

"Care for a brandy?" Kenneth offered, pouring himself one.

"Not for me, thanks," I replied.

Dastrie and Muriel similarly declined.

Our conversation during dinner had drifted in desultory fashion from the Rowlings's children's accomplishments to Frank's untimely death to the absence of any weather such as we knew it back east to, well, nothing at all. The two younger members of the family had been packed off to a friend's house for the night, and the catering crew would depart the premises very shortly.

"Have you made any progress investigating my father's death?" Mrs. Rowlings wanted to know.

"Well, I think I now have some better idea of what actually happened there," I stated. "Of course, I'm still waiting for confirmation of several details, but I should be able to file a report with the Sheriff's Department by next week."

"Really?" Kenneth posed. "What are you going to say?"

"It wasn't an accident, for one thing," I indicated. "Frank's car couldn't have wound up where it was by happenstance. We also have a report of another vehicle being present on the scene at the same time, plus at least two other persons who haven't been accounted for. All of this was missed by the investigating deputies, but was confirmed by witnesses.

"Also, Frank himself wasn't drunk, as the initial reports indicated, but was apparently doused with a bottle of booze by whoever else was at the scene. He was actually riding in the right-hand seat of the automobile; by inference, another individual had to have driven him there. The question naturally arises: since we know that Frank exited the vehicle before it was struck by the train, why didn't he save himself? The engineer reported that he was weaving back and forth on the track, as if he didn't have complete control of his body. What other conditions might have caused such incapacity in a man of his age?"

"Well, uh, I'm sure I don't know," Rowlings replied. "There are many possibilities."

"But you were his regular physician: you'd know the nature of his ailments if anyone would. Remind us again about the state of his health during this past year."

"He was, uh, he was in pretty decent shape for a man of his age," the doctor indicated, "except for his diabetes, of course: he had to exercise and regulate his diet to control his blood sugar levels."

"You said earlier that he also took insulin."

"Yes," Rowlings agreed, "sometimes the disease progresses to a point where it can't be controlled in any other way."

"You also told us that Frank disliked having to inject himself."

"That's correct. Almost always the injections were performed by Cyndi or Muriel, or sometimes by me or my nurse, depending on where he was and who was available."

"How many times a day was the insulin administered?"

"Uh, optimally, Mr. Havens should have received three such treatments daily: at breakfast, dinner, and just before bedtime," the MD replied.

"What would have been the effect of missing one of those injections?" I posed.

"Why, nothing under normal circumstances," Rowlings said. "I mean, in the long term, of course, the absence of regular doses would have increased his blood sugar levels to the point where he could have suffered blindness, nerve damage, kidney failure, and other severe consequences. But the absence of one shot wouldn't have been at all noticeable, either to him or to anyone else."

"And if too much insulin was used?"

Rowlings suddenly swallowed audibly and then gulped down the rest of his drink. He immediately poured himself another and took a second large swig.

"Well, Doctor Rowlings?"

"Uh, he might have suffered a low-sugar episode."

"What does that mean exactly?" I wanted to know.

"In normal people the body regulates the release of glucose into the bloodstream on a steady basis to provide energy for basic functions. The hormone called insulin is used to control this release. In diabetics this mechanism is damaged; the body has lost its ability to govern the amount of sugar circulating at any one time. If it goes too low—if too much insulin is present—the person can enter an irreversible coma or suffer from other organ damage."

"What might be the symptoms of a low-sugar episode?"

"There are many possible reactions," the doctor countered. "Different people respond in different ways."

"But what's the normal response?" I pressed.

"Uh, the patient might appear to be slightly inebriated."

"In other words, he'd look like he was drunk. He'd stagger, have difficulty comprehending the situation, sweat, display clammy hands and extremities, and be wholly unable to cope with a crisis."

"Yes, that could happen, but…"

"Those are the usual symptoms of an overdose of insulin, Dr. Rowlings, as you well know. Who injected Mr. Havens with his second dosage on the final day of his life?"

"It wasn't me!" Rowlings exclaimed. "I had nothing to do with it!"

I looked at Muriel. Her eyes met mine, and then she dropped her head.

"I did it," she finally admitted.

"And he trusted you to do so, didn't he?" I pressed.

"Yes."

"And you gave him an overdose."

She sighed: "Yes."

"Why, Muriel?"

"It's a long, sad story," she finally said. "You wouldn't understand, Van."

"No, I don't think I would," I replied, "but let me just see if I can fill in some of the blanks.

"A decade ago Kenneth Rowlings was well launched on a promising career as a physician catering to high society. His connection to the Havens family, and Frank's willingness to refer clients to him, had basically secured his future. He even did the patriotic thing by joining the Army.

"But you were never satisfied with the *status quo*, were you, Kenneth? You always had to have more. Never mind that you were blessed beyond most men. It wasn't sufficient for you.

"You got bored with hospital life. Rehabilitating our brave soldiers wasn't enough for you. You started dallying with several willing nurses. One of them became pregnant. She agreed to your proposal that you take care of the situation with an abortion. You agreed to buy her silence with a thousand dollars. Her roommate assisted with the procedure, which was done off-base, and everything was going fine until the middle of the next morning, when she started bleeding.

"I don't think that she even understood what was happening until it was too late. Her girlfriend was supposed to stay with her for a couple of days to make sure she was all right, but she'd gone off with her beau for the night and wasn't there to check on her roommate. I know from my own experience in the war that when you're warm and comfortable and sleeping in a bed, you sometimes don't even notice extraneous bleeding until it's well advanced. Blood's the same temperature as your body, and unless it cools, you can lose an awful lot of it without even realizing the fact. Maybe she just drifted off into a coma, or maybe she woke up suddenly and tried to do something about it, but was too befuddled to call for help.

"In any event, she died, and that changed everything, didn't it, Kenneth? Because you and she were a known couple on base, and even though she'd died in town, once the cause of death had been established, suspicion would immediately have fallen upon you. And that would have been the end of your promising career and life.

"So when the girlfriend discovered her roommate dead the next morning, she immediately telephoned you. You found some excuse for leaving base, cleaned up the mess in the hotel room, bought off the other girl (she would have been charged as an accomplice in any case if the truth had ever come out), and stashed the body somewhere else, where it wasn't found for many days, maybe even a week or two. By then the medical evidence had been fudged enough that the event couldn't be specifically linked to Kenneth Rowlings—although your superior believed otherwise. He accused you of the crime, and said that he was going to make your life an unholy hell until you confessed.

"So you went to your father-in-law and told him that you were being unjustly persecuted, and when Frank investigated, as he would, it seemed that this was the case. Pincus was inventing petty crimes to lay at your feet, trying to frame you for things that basically weren't your fault or responsibility.

"That's where I came in. Frank came to me and I got you reassigned—oh, I can see by your expression that you didn't know *that*, did you? Well, that's what actually happened.

"So you came to California and you liked what you saw, and you eventually brought your family out here. The terrible past just faded away, and everything was fine and dandy—until, that is, you got bored again.

"Then you started gambling, just a little at first, but increasingly more as time went by. You were taking greater and greater risks, and spending more and more of your family's wealth. Muriel eventually had to prevail upon her father's generosity in order to cover your debts— perhaps several times. Finally, Frank decided to relocate here himself, and then things began getting a little dicey, didn't they?

"Frank was no fool. He realized very quickly that you were involved with some very seamy characters, and he put you on a tight budget—too tight for your now inflamed tastes. You had to raise money somehow, so you started doing abortions again. It was quick and easy cash and the girls couldn't fight back, particularly when you routed them through Madame Heike's establishment. Some of them never emerged from that hell-hole. You and the Madame soon became business partners. You'd keep the girls healthy and help supply her with an unending source of new slaves, and she'd lend you money when necessary to meet your increasing obligations.

"Then—and this is mere speculation on my part—Frank discovered what you were doing. Maybe one of the girls came to him, or maybe he just kept his ear close to the ground, so to speak. He was no dummy, and being in the newspaper business, he would have quickly established sources everywhere in the community. He gave you an ultimatum: stop performing abortions or he'd turn you in. Havens was too righteous a gentleman to condone such abuse of human innocents.

"You panicked. Playtime was suddenly over! And you still owed thousands of dollars to individuals who were not going to allow you much leeway over repayment. You *had* to raise a large sum right away.

"But Frank wasn't at all sympathetic to your plight, was he? I think he told you, 'Enough is enough!' So you went to Muriel and begged her to intercede, as she always had in the past; and she took your case to her father, expecting him to bail you out once again. For the very first time in her life, her father turned her down. He stood on basic principle: he could not—would not—allow these crimes to continue."

I was watching their faces all the while that I was talking, and I knew that what I said was the plain truth: I could see it in their expressions. They looked like little kids who'd suddenly been caught with their hands in the cookie jar. But they *weren't* little kids: they were adults who'd been playing games with people's lives. They'd hurt folks just to save face. They should have known better. Their rich, over-pampered existences weren't worth the pain they'd caused even one of those girls, not to mention Frank. I continued with my narrative:

"What confused me was the notation in Frank's diary that he was supposed to meet and phone someone named 'RN.' But that was you, Muriel. You'd worked as a nurse for Kenneth when he'd first established himself here, and he got to calling you Arnie—short for 'RN,' or registered nurse—and Frank picked it up himself when he settled here.

"When Muriel returned from Frank's office and told you the bad news, you lost your temper, Dr. Rowlings. You informed your wife in very clear and unmistakable language just what her options were. Everything was on the line: your marriage, the business, your reputation in the community, even the lives of your children. Havens had all that money—and none of it was yours. You and she stood to inherit at least half of his estate, of that you were certain. It would solve all your problems. All he had to do was to die.

"He was old, after all. You expect old people to die. And it was the simplest thing, really. He was always getting these insulin injections, and he didn't like doing them himself. You could substitute something lethal, and he'd never be the wiser. But then you thought: what if there was an autopsy? What if the symptoms seemed odd? What if the police actually investigated?

"Then the obvious occurred to you: you didn't have to give him a *different* drug. Insulin would do quite well indeed. You'd increase the dosage and he'd go into hypoglycemic shock. Maybe the bugger'd just die in his sleep. But the old man proved more resilient than you thought, and he started getting suspicious of his intermittent 'spells.' He insisted on only his wife giving him the injections. You had to put him in a situation where Cyndi wouldn't be available.

"And that was your idea, wasn't it, Muriel? Kenneth certainly didn't have enough imagination to come up with a notion like that. After all, who'd ever suspect a loving daughter who was just trying to help dear old dad? You didn't have to kill him; you just had to make him appear drunk. Then he'd have a little accident with his car, and nobody would be the wiser.

"That's the way it played out, too, until Cyndi asked me to investigate. She smelled something rotten in the icebox. She knew things weren't right—and so did Frank, of course, although I don't think he ever would have believed that his own flesh and blood would turn against him. After everything he'd done for the both of you, you repaid him with murder.

"You knew about the threatening notes he was receiving—he'd told you, Muriel—so you sent him another one saying, 'I KNOW WHEN YOU DIE!' Then if the police ever had gotten suspicious, you could have blamed Frank's death on The Phantom's Phantom—or maybe on The Phantom himself. Because you knew my identity, Muriel: Frank had given you the secret many years ago, with my approval. He'd thought that it was only fair that you knew why I couldn't marry you, so you could get on with your own life."

"Oh, I got on with my life, all right," Muriel replied. "I found myself a real ringer: Dr. Kenneth Mortimer Rowlings, a good-looking charmer with a heart full of tin and a bona fide professional degree from the University of Grenada. Yeah, I really won the jackpot there."

"He gave you two great children, if nothing else," I commented. "You could have divorced him at any time, my dear."

"What would my friends have said? Divorce simply wasn't an option, and when Daddy wouldn't pay Frank's debts off, the local bosses made it clear that those debts would have to be accounted for very soon, with interest, or my two babies would be violated in the worse possible way. I had no choice. Something had to be done.

"Daddy was old and set in his ways. He would have died soon anyway. When measured against our lives and those of the next generation, well, there was no other possibility, really. He became expendable, just as I was expendable to you, Van."

"I never treated you like that," I replied.

"No, you treated me *worse!*" she spat. "You treated me like dirt, Van. You stepped on my ego, you ignored my worth, and you violated my trust. When I learned who you really were, I became physically ill. I vomited, over and over again. You know why? Do you understand why? I *loved* you, Van, and it was suddenly obvious that you didn't give a tinker's damn about Muriel Marie Havens. I was just a convenient cover for you, that's all, just another pretty face to parade around at society gigs. I was crushed, completely demoralized, and Dr. Kenneth Rowlings was the result. I discovered him on the rebound, before I was able to make good judgments again. It was all your fault, all of it.

"So don't go lecturing *me* about morality and right and wrong. You've killed hundreds, maybe thousands, of people, in your personal vendetta against crime. How many of those individuals were innocent, Van? How do you know they were all guilty? How many really deserved to die? How many bereaving wives and kids and brothers and sisters and parents did you leave lying by the wayside? Do you even know? Can you even guess?

"My father didn't deserve to die, I know that. But all of us die eventually, and it was his turn. He died so we could live, so my children could live. I'm sorry that he had to die, I truly am, but what else could I do?"

"But how could you watch him die, Muriel?" I pressed. "How could you coldly inject Frank with an overdose of insulin, and then drive him to that naked corner in the middle of nowhere? How could you leave him sitting in the car when you knew that a train was coming, when you knew that he'd see the engine rolling down those tracks towards him, and understand full well the extent to which he'd been betrayed? How cruel do you have to be to commit patricide?"

She starting sobbing then, and I almost felt sorry for what I'd done to her—almost, but not quite.

"Somebody has to pay for what's happened here," I continued. "An eye for an eye: one of you has to go down for this."

That got their attention, front and center.

"You have forty-eight hours to decide what you're going to do and who's going to take the rap—and for what crimes. If I don't hear from you by Monday morning, I'll go to the DA myself, and present him with my evidence and conclusions. Then *he* can decide your fate.

"However, I won't make your children orphans. One of you can stay home while the other goes to prison. That's the best—that's the *only*—deal that I have on the table, folks. And *please* don't try to jigger things yourselves: I've cached my information in several safe places; if anything happens to either of us in the interim, you'll both be fingered."

I stood up.

"We'll show ourselves out. Thank you for a lovely dinner."

Then we left.

We were rolling down the hill towards Barton Street when my hands started shaking. I just couldn't control them.

My companion put her arms around me and held me to her breast.

"You're so very cold," she said.

"That's what I'm afraid of," I responded. I lifted my head and looked at her straight in the eyes: "You need to understand something, Dastrie. There's a part of me that's as black as the deepest coal pit, that's as icy as the South Pole, and that has done—and will do—things that you can only imagine in your worst nightmares. I'm exactly what Muriel accused me of: a widow-maker, an orphan-monger, a slayer of souls, a killing machine. I'm all of those things and more. Don't ever forget who I am and what I've done."

"I can live with that if you can, Richard," she stated.

"I don't know if I can," I whispered. "I don't know, Dastrie."

XII.

"I KNOW WHO YOU WERE!"
▲
No mask like open truth to cover lies,
As to go naked is the best disguise.
—William Congreve
▼

SAN BERNARDINO, CALIFORNIA
SATURDAY, 31 OCTOBER 1953
ALL HALLOWS EVE

The phone rang promptly at seven the next morning. Unusually, we'd both slept in that day, and I was sound asleep when the call came through.

"Yeah," I managed to growl into the receiver.

"It's Muriel, Van."

I was instantly awake, and so was Dastrie beside me.

"What do you want, Muriel?"

"Frank's taken a gun and gone to that whore's place in San Bernardino. He said something about collecting what was owed to him. We had this enormous argument last night after you left. He wanted to kill you. I told him that wouldn't solve the problem. I didn't know about the abortions, really I didn't, and I said I didn't approve of such things. He just laughed at me, Van. 'What do you think paid for all that furniture?' he countered, pointing at the sofa: 'That's one little job, right there.' It just made me sick.

"He finally agreed to go to the police with what he'd done to those girls, provided that Madame Heike was charged too. He really doesn't like that woman very much.

"But this morning he said that she still owed him ten thousand dollars, and he intended to collect every last dime before he turned himself in. You've got to go down there, Van. I'm afraid of what he might do in this frame of mind."

Sure she was! I didn't believe a word of it. What'd happened to the sweet and innocent kid that I'd known twenty years ago? Where was the girl who'd cried over the loss of a fledging that she'd found one day under an old elm tree?

105

Wherever that woman had gone, she sure as hell wasn't coming back again. I didn't trust this new Muriel for an instant. But I told her that I'd see what I could do.

"You'd better stay here," I told Dastrie. "This could get nasty."

"Not a chance," she responded. "You get dressed and shaved while I phone Tigre."

We were ready for action twenty minutes later, but it was still close to eight by the time we reached South "D" Street. Cop cars were littered everywhere: it might have been a used car lot with hood lights. The city police had already established a perimeter around the old mansion that doubled as Heike's fancy cathouse. William Jardine was on scene as an observer, so I buttonholed him.

"What's going on here, sheriff?" I asked.

"So it's you, Van Loan: I could've figured you'd show up. You always seem to appear every goddam place there's trouble.

"Someone's holding Heike the Whore hostage, I haven't been told who. Far as I'm concerned, he can goddam slit the damned bitch's throat then and there, and call the trash collectors."

"I thought you lawmen were some of her best customers," I observed, trying to be helpful.

"I don't claim we're not," the officer said, "but what my men do and what I do are two different things. Heike's at the root of a lot of the corruption and crime in this town, and it's way, way past time that her bunch get the royal boot out of San Berdoo. I think this may just do it."

Just then a city cop sauntered over.

"Who's the john?" I asked him.

"Some quack named Rowlings," the policeman noted. "He provides health services for the Madame's 'employees'."

"Dr. Rowlings, huh?" I replied. "Frank Havens's son-in-law is Kenneth Rowlings. It's not that common a name. I know him, gentlemen."

"Why am I not surprised?" Jardine countered. "What d'ya want *me* to do about it?"

"Well, guys, I could go over there and see what he wants. He might listen to me when he wouldn't to you."

"Richard, he'll *kill* you!" Dastrie gasped into my ear.

"Gee, that's even better! We might get two for one this time," Jardine indicated. "I'll go talk to the goddam police chief."

He was back in a couple of minutes: "You wanna go, Van Loan, you go right ahead. Nobody here's going to goddam stop you."

"*No*, Richard!" my companion pleaded, holding tightly to my arm.

"I've got to do this," I told her, shaking off the restraint.

Then I sauntered right across that wide open space to the wrought iron fence and gate. It creaked loudly as I swung open the portal.

"That's far enough, Van!" a voice shouted from the doorway.

"I just want to talk, Kenneth," I yelled back.

"We talked enough last night," came the reply. "I don't have anything else to say."

"Why don't you let Heike go," I said.

"Let her go? You crazy, Van? She was why I got into this mess in the first place. She lent me money, and then I had to pay her off by finding new meat for her 'shop,' and keep them cleaned up and working. You think that was fun for me? Even when the debt was paid off, she held me fast by the short and narrow, Van. She said she'd leak information to the police if I ever stopped.

"She owes me over ten grand now, you believe that? I only had to break two of her fingers before she opened the safe. There were fifty big ones in there, Van. She was rolling in it, just like Frank. I have nothing and they have everything. It just isn't fair."

"Let her go, Kenneth. She'll be arrested, and once she's convicted, she'll serve her time—probably the rest of her life. She'll be punished by the law."

"Oh, she's being punished, all right. I've made sure of that. I just followed your example, Van. So get the hell out of Dodge: I've got nothing more to say to you. I'm sure not going to prison, and I'm not going to surrender to anyone either. I don't care what you and Muriel want. I'm through listening to either of you."

"Let the girls go then," I begged. "They've done nothing to deserve this."

"They're just dumb broads," the doctor retorted. "They seduce and entice and corrupt us. They don't contribute anything worthwhile to the world. The whores deserve what they get."

"No, Kenneth, they don't," I replied. "They never had a chance, and you know it. They were innocent when you brought them here."

"They were *never* innocent, Van. They were knocked up, all of them. They'd already opened their legs to some pimple-pocked boy, and they paid the price for their rampant promiscuity. I had to cut their brats out of each of them."

"And what if your daughter had been one of them, Kenneth? What then? They've done nothing to you. Let them go. Remember the Hippocratic oath you swore: 'first, do no harm'."

There was a long pause, and then I heard a muffled voice from within ordering the young women to "Get your asses down here right away, all of you!"

"They're coming out!" Rowlings shouted out the door.

The girls almost ran down the steps in their terror, sobbing and shaking and quite obviously scared to death.

They were quickly surrounded by police matrons, who started putting them in official cars to be taken to the County Hospital for examination.

I followed them back across that lonely road. There was nothing more that I could do to save Kenneth Rowlings from himself. Dastrie embraced me as I reached the safety of the barricades.

As soon as the girls were clear, the Chief of Police picked up a megaphone and yelled, "You've got five minutes to give yourself up, Rowlings. Throw out your gun and come out with your hands up!"

There was no reply, nor did I expect any. I knew how this would go down. When the ultimatum expired, the police shot half a dozen tear gas canisters through the windows. Rowlings dived out the front door onto the porch, rolling once and shooting wildly as he came erect. A dozen police weapons returned fire, and the body toppled over the rail. Kenneth Rowlings had finally been called to account.

The Phantom would have been proud, but I didn't know how Richard Van Loan felt. I didn't really have the stomach for this sort of thing any longer. Maybe I *was* getting old, or maybe my association with Dastrie was beginning to change my basic instincts. I didn't miss the old feelings at all.

When we got back to the Hot Springs Hotel and Spa, I phoned Muriel with the bad news.

"I've already heard," she stated. "You satisfied now, Van? Has the piper been paid sufficiently to quench your blood lust?"

"It's enough," I admitted.

"What about Daddy's death?"

"That was an accident: the sheriff said so, and who am I to contradict an official investigation? But I never want to see you again, Muriel, not ever."

"But you have to, Van. There's still the scattering of Daddy's ashes tomorrow."

"You're going to collapse from grief over Kenneth's passing, Muriel, and you won't be able to attend. Because if you *are* there, *my dear old friend*, I'll make certain that Cyndi knows what really happened to Frank, and I'll leave your fate in her hands. Is that what you want?"

She couldn't reply for a full minute.

"You're a real son-of-a-bitch, Van," she finally choked out. "I hate you."

Then she hung up.

I knew then that she'd stay away from Frank's service. I didn't want his memory sullied by the presence of his killer, even if that fact wasn't known to anyone but me and Dastrie. It just wasn't right.

Dastrie wanted me to go down to lunch, but I couldn't even contemplate food at a time like this. I was thoroughly enervated and vaguely nauseous, so much so that I insisted on taking a nap. My lovely girl, bless her to the gods, didn't say a word, but just drew the curtains, put the "DO NOT DISTURB!" sign on the door, and cuddled up next to me. We had a few hours to spare before we had to get ready for the ball.

When I arose, relaxed and refreshed, I knew I was ready for our final challenge. I went through an abbreviated regimen of my exercises, took a quick shower, and then called "Room Service." I needed some energy for the events yet to come.

So we ordered the breakfast that we'd missed that morning, three eggs sunny side up over some *linguica* sausage and sourdough toast, all washed down with a tall glass of freshly squeezed orange juice and a cup of hot, unsweetened tea. I felt much restored afterwards.

Then Dastrie went back to her room to get dressed, and I hunted up the dark suit and coat and hat that I'd sported as The Phantom Detective, together with the mask that completed the costume. When I looked in the mirror, I gasped at the memories that the outfit brought back to me.

A few moments later, there was a soft rap on the door. When I let Dastrie in, I just started laughing. Staring back at me was a soft green velvet version of my outfit, complete with low-brimmed hat and the same style mask framing her sparkling eyes.

"I thought you'd appreciate this," she commented, pirouetting so I could get the full effect.

"It's delightful!" I exclaimed, shaking my head in wonderment.

This woman always had the ability to surprise and please.

"I also brought these"—she held out a half-dozen red armbands. "They'll help identify us in the crowd."

"What a great idea," I agreed, slipping one onto her arm and then another onto mine.

One by one our team appeared, and they were all dressed exactly alike, each and every one. This was Dastrie's doing, I knew, a kind of small statement on her part, but one I didn't mind in the slightest. Zinc handed out the guns and clips to each person who needed one.

We changed back into normal clothing and went down to dinner together around six, enjoying a leisurely repast of roast beef and vegetables and mixed fruit. The party was supposed to start around nine, as soon as the tables and chairs had been cleared from the Palmatoria Room.

After dinner, we assembled again in my room and donned our costumes anew. Then the rest of the group gathered 'round while I gave them my final disposition.

"Be careful," I cautioned. "The Phantom's Phantom will certainly be present, but he may have accomplices, and they'll be armed, I'm sure. Watch over each other, and keep an eye on me and Dastrie. Follow our lead when the time comes. And please don't take any chances: we don't want any bystanders hurt."

The festivities had already started when we made our appearance, each person scattering to his or her predetermined position in the large room. I'd placed them along the sides so that they could easily see each other.

I had no idea what to expect, but I was ready (I hoped) for anything.

But nothing happened to us, at least initially. The crowd grew rapidly, as "pretty young things" dressed in almost nothing but elaborate masks and pastel dresses and colorful capes and lace swirled this way and that, some serving drinks and *hors d'œuvres*, others just mingling with the guests. I had no way of distinguishing between those actually staying at the hotel and those who'd crashed the party, either by invitation or by design. An orchestra in one corner played gypsy airs and other curious, even wild tunes (some of which I didn't recognize), filled with flights of violin fancy and high-flying flings of flaunting flutes.

The lights in the Palmatoria Room had gradually dimmed, leaving just a few flickering artificial candles to illuminate the mass of heaving, moving bodies. It was impossible for me to see past my immediate group, and I realized suddenly that all our plans had gone awry.

"Care to dance?" one of the women asked.

She didn't wait for my reply, but grabbed my arms and spun me into the maelstrom.

"Who're you supposed to be?" she shouted in my ear. "I'm the Lady of Spain."

It was difficult to hear anyone over the incessant din.

"The Phantom," I replied.

"Oh, the Phantom of the Opera: I think I saw the movie. He had a mask just like that."

"No," I said, "The Phantom Detective."

"The Phantom what?" she yelled back. "Who's that?"

"Never mind," I replied.

I broke away from her as soon as I dared, but was immediately snatched up by another young woman, this one slimmer than the last. She'd painted her face like a cat's, and wore pointed ears.

"Meow," she purred, as she held me close, running her tongue over her bright red lips, and actually poking it out to lick the tip of my nose. "Why, it's Mr. Van Loan!" she said. "I KNOW WHO YOU WERE! my dear old Phantom."

Then she laughed, a wicked little lie, and abruptly spun away from me. I tried chasing after her, but there were too many people in the way. I kept bumping into foxes and bears and Marie Antoinettes and once even an old froggie named Dougie, but never one of my own crew.

Then a man materialized right in front of me. He was sporting a coat, a hat, a cape, and a mask identical to mine, but all in white, where mine was uniformly black.

"You don't blend in very well," I commented, bowing my head in acknowledgement of the pantomime.

"Ah, Mr. Phantom, I don't really want to blend in," the man stated. "Shall we dance?"

Before I could respond, he yanked my hands and pulled me into the maw. 'Round and 'round we turned, until my head starting spinning with the exertion, and then he slowed the pace again, as we pranced into a corner where the racket wasn't so loud.

Then he began chanting: """The time has come," the Walrus said, "to talk of many things: Of shoes—and ships—and sealing wax—Of cabbages—and kings—And why the sea is boiling hot—And whether pigs have wings."""

"Lewis Carroll," I stated.

"Or Charles Lutwidge Dodgson, by any other name," he noted. """But wait a bit," the Oysters cried, "Before we have our chat; For some of us are out of breath, And all of us are fat!"""

I knew "The Walrus and the Carpenter" as well as anyone: """I weep for you," the Walrus said: "I deeply sympathize."""

"Actually, I doubt that very much, Mr. Phantom," my adversary noted. "In any event, even if you *had* reformed, such sentiments come way too late in our relationship to make any real difference."

"I kept your brother out of jail, Riley McCarty," I stated. "I didn't have to do that, as you well know."

"But you didn't keep *me* from serving time, Richard Van Loan."

"You were guilty as charged," I indicated. "You stole a quarter million dollars. You were justly convicted by a jury of your peers in a court of law, and you were sentenced to prison for your crimes."

"And while I was incarcerated in Sing Sing, my mother died of grief and my father perished in poverty while trying to raise funds for my defense. They don't even have a tombstone to mark their final resting place: we couldn't afford one. My two younger brothers and my sister worked themselves to the bone at menial jobs, and I endured a decade of abuse at the hands of my fellow inmates.

"But I never lost my faith, Van Loan, never! I prayed to Almighty God every day for my deliverance, and He told me that once I'd been sufficiently chastised for my sins, He would free me to do His work, to exact vengeance upon those who transgressed against His Holy

Law. Two days after the tenth anniversary of my conviction, I was being transported to another prison when the convict bus broke down. The other prisoners overpowered and beat the guards and escaped. *I*, however, chose not to leave, but instead used the radio to bring medical help to the men who'd been injured. The others were all caught. But…"

"…The governor pardoned you, and you were released from jail last summer," I said. "Yes, I've already heard the news, McCarty. And when you got out, you started looking for me, because you blamed me for all your troubles."

"No!" came the response. "I did what I did, and I was justly punished by God for my sins. I accept that now. No, I blame *you*, Van Loan, for what happened to my family. *You* could have saved them."

"I didn't know," I responded.

"But I wrote to you asking for help," McCarty stated. "Several times I sent you messages in care of Frank Havens, since I didn't know how else to reach you."

"I never received them," I indicated, "and I doubt that Frank did either. Or if he did, he probably thought that that they were just crank letters. Both of us got many such missives over the years."

"I wrote you!" he repeated. "You should have responded. You should have known, Van Loan. You could have saved them, just by lifting your little finger. You never once thought about the consequences of what you did to me and the others. You never considered the collateral damage."

"You're right," I conceded, "but it makes no difference now. You used Frank to locate me."

"Yes, and when Mr. Havens suddenly died, I knew that God had spoken once again. He struck down mine enemy without me lifting even my littlest finger. My power was waxing in His Light."

"But you threatened Frank," I replied.

"Yes," he agreed, "but I didn't kill him or anyone else either, well, except for the minister, and that was an accident. He just got in the way of the bullet. God told me, though, that He had His reasons for harvesting that particular soul. The man was a hypocrite who molested the choir boys."

"What do you want from me, Riley?"

"I've already told you: I want to see you suffer. I want your family to experience the same pain that mine did. I don't want to kill you. I just want to be The Phantom's Phantom."

"One Phantom is probably enough for this world," I noted. "I can't let you do that."

"Well, then," my enemy responded, "catch me if you can!"

Without warning he grabbed a drink off a nearby tray and dashed it in my eyes, temporarily blinding me with the stinging liquor, just for a second. When I looked around again, he was gone, merged back into the orgy of inane inconsequence that obscured all possible discernment in that dim, dank hall.

A moment later I found Zinc planted along one wall and described the two individuals that I'd seen.

"They're four of them, probably including Laz, and they're likely armed," I indicated. "I want them caught. Have you seen any of the others?"

"Nobody, boss," he said.

"Then follow me," I ordered.

Fifteen minutes of active searching rounded up both Nate and Tigre, but Laz and Dastrie were missing in the *mêlée*. By this time it was after ten, but the party showed no sign of breaking up, and I suspected that it would wend its weary way into the wee hours of All Saints' Day.

I pulled my trio of friends into the lobby, where it was a tad quieter.

"I'm worried about Miss Underhill," I told them. "It's not like her to just leave like that."

"Mr. Van Loan!" one of the desk clerks shouted, "message for you!"

He handed me another white envelope, another lie to read:

> *"Now stir the fire, and close the shutters fast,*
> *Let fall the curtains, wheel the sofa round,*
> *And, while the bubbling and loud-hissing urn*
> *Throws up a steamy column, and the cups,*
> *That cheer but not inebriate, wait on each,*
> *So let us welcome peaceful evening in.*
>   —The Phantom's Phantom"

"William Cowper," I muttered. "The man's a veritable quotation machine."

"But what does it mean?" Nate asked. "Look, there's something written on the other side!"

> *"Place me on Sunium's marble steep,*
> *Where nothing save the waves and I*
> *May hear our mutual murmurs sweep;*
> *There, swanlike, let me sing and die.*
> *A land of slaves shall ne'er be mine—*
> *Dash-trie yon cup of Samian wine!"*

"Now he's quoting Lord Byron," I stated. "Whatever he's done with her, we have till midnight to solve the puzzle. He's given us that much time. And I'd bet my life that it has something to do with the warm springs here."

I walked back to the check-out desk.

"Excuse me," I asked the clerk, "can you tell me the location of all the hot springs on the grounds?"

"Sorry, sir," came the reply, "I just work here on the weekends. I'm a student at the University of Redlands."

"Who else might know?"

"Probably the night manager, Mr. Bernard Rich," the clerk stated. "His office is down the corridor to the right."

"Thank you."

We found the door and rapped on it. When the man himself appeared, I posed the same question to him.

"We don't have a map as such, but I can tell you where they are," the supervisor indicated. "There's one located out at the northeastern end of the site, but it's completely overgrown with brush and inaccessible. We have a second spring that's been piled high with rocks to display to visitors out near the main entrance, and another near the terminus of the water train tracks, a fourth that heats the spa, a fifth for the mud bath pools, a sixth to warm the swimming pool, and a seventh buried under the hotel itself."

"Under the hotel?" I posed.

"Yes, the original building, a health resort, was erected over a large outflow of super-heated water, and featured hot baths and steam rooms and the associated massage and athletic equipment, state of the art for the time. This was back in the Gay Nineties.

"Although the caverns still exist, and can be accessed both externally and internally, they've been effectively closed off for decades. They were just too expensive to maintain as regular features for the guests, particularly once the mud baths, spa, and heated swimming pool were constructed. They're rented out on special occasions by pre-arrangement with the hotel."

"Is anyone using them now?" I wanted to know.

"No one's leased the facilities for years. The Navy employed them during World War II for rehabilitation of injured servicemen, but to my knowledge they haven't been rented more than two or three times since then. Most of the staff doesn't even know they exist."

"How can I access the caves?"

"You can't!" the man replied. "These things have to be arranged well in advance, because the rooms need to be cleaned first. We can't just allow anyone down there. There are liability issues, you know."

"How about a thousand dollars—and we take our own chances."

"Uh, sir, I really can't. I mean, I don't have the authority…"

"Two thousand." I offered.

114

"Sir, this is foolishness."

"Five thousand!"

"I'll go find the key and a release form for you to sign."

Then he gave us directions on how to locate the door in the basement area that led to the hotel underworld.

"Meanwhile," I stated, "please call the Sheriff's Department. Tell them that Van Loan needs their assistance right away. Make sure they get that message exactly as I've stated it."

"But, sir, I really don't think...."

However, we were already striding down the hallway to the lobby. We found our way through a maze of doors and stairs and corridors, until we came to the nondescript entrance to the Steam Caverns. As I half expected, the padlock had already been forced.

"Check your weapons, gentlemen," I ordered, and everyone carefully examined their loads and clips and flicked off their safeties.

"Ready?" I asked.

When each of them nodded in turn, I carefully eased the metal door open a crack, and stuck my pistol through.

"Blam!" came the sound, and I could feel the shot carom off the structure.

"Duck!" I yelled, and crashed past the barrier at a low angle.

"Zing!" I felt the second bullet scoot right past my head, the whine of its passage sounding like the high-pitched flight of a mosquito.

I fired blindly into the blackness in front of me. I flattened myself to the floor, with my crew sprawling themselves protectively to either side. We saw the flash of a third shot, and immediately returned fire in tandem. There was a scream of pain, and the enemy's weapon clattered to the floor.

"I've been hit!" a man yelled.

"Can you move?" came the retort.

"Barely!"

"Then get yourself out of there!" Riley McCarty ordered.

The injured shooter must have been either Laz O'Riley or his younger brother, Patrick McCarty. Whoever it was, I could hear him grunting in agony as he slowly retreated back into the depths.

"Give it up, Riley!" I yelled into the darkness. "The cops are on their way."

"They'll never catch me," he replied. "God's on our side, Van Loan, and He's going to punish you!"

"God helps those who help themselves," I stated. "Let the girl go!"

"Why should I? She's your family, Van Loan. She's got to pay for what you did to mine."

"She's innocent, McCarty. Release her and I'll let you go."

"And I'm supposed to believe that, Van Loan? 'Sides, she's not all *that* innocent. She's killed a dozen people. That's a lot more than I have. You didn't know that, did you? She's not exactly a babe in the woods, if you know what I mean."

"My word is good. Let her go and I'll let you go."

"No way, José, to use the local vernacular. My little Laurella is just starting to have some fun with her, aren't you, my dear?"

"Oh, yes, dear brother," came the voice of the cat-woman that I'd encountered at the masquerade.

Then I heard a scream of agony, long and loud and lonely.

"Why, I think that was Dastrie Lee Underhill calling to you, Van Loan. Was it the voice of love or the cry of the loon? I wonder."

"Bastard!" I exclaimed. "Harm her and I'll never stop looking for you, Riley—or your siblings either. I'll track you down one by one and kill you very, very slowly. That's a promise—and I keep my promises, as I've already said."

"Ha! I don't care anymore, Van Loan!" McCarty warbled. "I'm The Phantom's Phantom! I'm the Hand of Almighty God! He'll protect me and mine! You can't touch me!"

"Well, I sure as hell am going to try!" I shouted back.

I started moving forward then, and my three compatriots, bless them all, followed right along behind me. Not one of them hesitated to put himself into harm's way to save one of their own. They all knew just what had to be done. I understood then that, if we managed to survive this long night, the organization that I'd created would continue going long after I'd departed the scene.

Deeper and deeper we wended our way into the earth, down a long stairwell constructed of stone, feeling our way from one place to the next. We had to move very slowly, because I was afraid of traps—and indeed, I located a trip wire right at the bottom of that final flight. It was probably attached to a grenade or something similar.

I whispered to each of them in turn, and we slowly, carefully lifted our legs over and past the hazard until we reached the bottom of the cavern. A long, dimly lit corridor stretched into the far distance to either side. Our view was partially obstructed by clouds of steam continually wafting their way into the hall from the baths themselves. Everywhere water dripped from the ceiling, and the old brick-and-tile surface of the structure was slick with mildew. We would have to be very careful where and how we stepped.

I put two of us facing in either direction.

"Psst!" Zinc said, grabbing my shoulder and pointing down at the floor.

I could see some small dark spots trailing off into the distance to the left.

"Blood!" I hissed, and motioned the rest of them to follow.

Another shot blared from the darkness, and Nate suddenly cried out in pain, falling to the floor.

"My leg!" he exclaimed.

"Stay here!" I ordered. "We'll come back for you."

I raised my right hand to the other two, showing one, two, and then three fingers. Then we charged down the corridor as fast as we could, pistols blazing our way.

I heard a body fall to the floor with a great "thump" and a rattle of the man's weapon as it skittered away from him across the wet tiles.

"Run, Laurella!" I heard McCarty order his sister, and I saw a figure rush out of a distant doorway and disappear into the mist.

I snapped a shot after her and I think I hit something too, because I heard a cry of pain, but she just kept on going. Then a small rectangular square of light appeared, and I realized that she'd opened an exit to the outside world at the far end.

Two more figures suddenly appeared in different doorways, one of them limping.

"Down!" I yelled, diving to the brick surface as the twin gunmen opened up on us.

We returned fire with deadly effect. One man toppled over, either dead or dying, and the other staggered back into a room on his left, holding one hand to his shoulder.

"Don't come any closer, Van Loan," he yelled, "or the dame dies now!"

"Let her go!" I repeated. "Let her go and I'll let you go, Riley."

"Give me a couple of minutes to think about it."

I suddenly realized that he was just buying time for his sister to escape.

The three of us moved down the corridor as quickly as we could without making any noise, and then I raised my hand to halt the others before the open doorway that led into the steam room.

"Cover me!" I ordered, and quickly slipped inside, diving to the floor.

I could hear the bullets zinging over my head. I rolled over once and then shot Riley McCarty twice between the eyes as I came erect. As he was falling to the surface—quite, quite dead—I was already rushing to the far end of the cavern.

Dastrie was tied to an old wooden bench there. It must have been close to 115° within the confines of the room. Steam was pouring continually out of a receptacle just in front of her. She was slumped in her restraints, her skin flushed with an unnatural rosy hue. One of her legs had been held over the outlet until it was scalded.

I slipped a knife out of my pocket and slit the ropes, making certain that her body didn't touch any of the hot pipes or steam jets. Then I gathered her in my arms, and with the help of my two compatriots, carried her back through our own version of Dante's *Inferno*.

We stopped briefly at the foot of the stairs to allow Zinc to disarm the grenade. He then picked up the injured Nate, and we found our way back up into the safety of the hotel.

The staff nurse permanently on duty at the resort took one look at my injured friends and immediately called an ambulance. They took them to the County Hospital. I rode in the back of the emergency vehicle with Dastrie and Nate, but she never regained consciousness. They toted them away into Emergency, leaving me standing there by myself, once again alone with the consequences of my actions.

About two the next morning one of the physicians approached me.

"Are you a relative of Miss Underhill?" he asked.

"Yes," I lied.

"She suffered a heat stroke and second-degree burns on her right leg. We're trying to cool her body down, injecting fluids into her as rapidly as she can handle them. She woke up briefly and asked for you, but we thought it better to sedate her until morning. Her leg is quite painful; we won't know the full extent of the injury for another day or two. There's nothing else you can do for her now, and I can't let you see her until tomorrow in any case."

"Will she be OK, doctor?"

"I don't know that yet," came the reply.

"Then I think I'll just sit here for a while," I said.

I was resting in a lounge area that had been established for the relatives of patients. The doctor just nodded his head once and went back to work.

I prayed then for the first time since I was a child. I begged God to spare Dastrie's life and to restore her health and well-being. I didn't care anything for myself: I just wanted to see her survive and be well.

I must have fallen asleep at some point.

"Mr. Van Loan?" the voice interjected, startling me awake.

Sometime in the last few hours the sun had reappeared. A different physician was now hovering over me.

"I'm happy to tell you that Miss Underhill is much improved this morning. We don't think the leg injury is serious, although it'll require further rehabilitation. We've managed to control her body temperature again, and we think she's on the road to recovery. Would you like to visit her?"

"Yes," I managed to gasp out.

I could hardly see to follow the doctor back down that long alabaster corridor. Something was blinding my eyes. I felt my cheek—it was damp. What the hell was the matter with me? What had changed?

Then I walked into that stark room in ICU and saw Dastrie Underhill sitting up in bed. I couldn't help myself. I just ran over and carefully—oh so gingerly—gathered her into my arms and thanked God that she was still alive.

We stayed in California for another month while my lover slowly regained her precious health. I attended the scattering of Frank's ashes later on Sunday, but neither Dastrie nor Muriel could be present, although the Rowlings's two children were both there to wish their grandfather into his eternal rest.

The following week I bought the Twin Pines Rancho from Cyndi Havens, and Dastrie and I honeymooned there instead of going on some distant voyage. Time enough for that later, I told her, when she had regained her usual good health.

Cyndi discovered that she had a knack for business, and did a better job of managing the newspaper even than Frank, who was, truth to tell, beginning to decline in his later years. I suspected that she'd be running a chain of such publications before she was through.

Madame Heike Helsinki (a pseudonym!) was charged with pandering, a misdemeanor, and served 100 days in the San Bernardino clink before being released on good behavior. She closed her business and retired to Carlsbad, somewhere down near San Diego. I knew that I eventually needed to pay her a little visit to square our accounts.

The bullet-ridden bodies of The Phantom's Phantom and his two younger brothers were indeed discovered sprawled in the Steam Caverns beneath the Hot Springs Hotel and Spa, but of Laurella McCarty there was no trace whatever, then or now. In Riley McCarty's vest pocket was a final scrawled message penned just for me:

"I UNDERSTAND YOUR PAIN!"

Maybe he did. Maybe he knew me better than I thought. Whenever I look in the mirror, I see this middle-aged man staring back at me with dark, dark circles under his eyes, and I know who The Phantom's Phantom *really* is.

And then Dastrie laughs at my pretensions, and the *doppelgänger* retreats back into the dark cave of my soul.

But you know something, dear friends?

He never goes completely away.

EPILOGUE

EXIT THE PHANTOM
▲
What's old collapses, times change,
And new life blossoms in the ruins.
—Friedrich von Schiller
▼

SAN BERNARDINO, CALIFORNIA
29 JANUARY 2006

"Professor Simmons?"

I'd fallen asleep in my office again, not a good sign for an aging English professor. I glanced at the page proofs before me and then marked my place. I'd almost finished reviewing *The Phantom's Phantom*. One or two more sessions would do it.

"Yes, Louise?" I replied.

"This came for you in the campus post."

She walked in and handed me a plain white envelope with my name scrawled on the front.

"I don't get much mail anymore," I said, "not since I retired."

"You don't mind, do you, professor?"

"Actually, Louise, I don't mind at all. I enjoy being on campus a few hours each week, and I like having my office, and I still relish teaching the odd course or two—but the pressure's gone. Besides, they have me editing a cookbook now!"

"A cookbook! When did this happen?"

"The dean called me yesterday. They're in a bind, and even though I can't boil an egg myself, they seem to think me amply qualified for the task."

"That's marvelous. I'd be happy to contribute a recipe," she offered.

"Why, thank you, Louise. I hope you will."

After she'd departed, I slit open the envelope. A three-by-five-inch white card popped out.

"I KNOW WHO YOU ARE!" it said.

"What!" I exclaimed out loud. "This isn't possible."

I looked around the room, but there was nothing and nobody to be seen, of course.

Then I thought very, very carefully about what I'd uncovered in the secret room on the Long Island estate of my late great-uncle Percy, and reviewed the steps that I'd taken to verify some of the events.

I didn't and don't know what Richard Van Loan's real name was—I could never find it written anywhere in Percy's records. I did verify that some of the physical sites described in the book, or at least their analogues, existed in 1953. One of the local newspapers in Redlands had indeed been purchased a few years before that date by a New York publisher who retired to the West Coast, but in real life he'd died peacefully in his sleep.

The names of the characters in the story didn't fit anyone living or dead at the time, other than the celebrities whom everyone would recognize.

I did drive out to Twin Pines Rancho and discovered a rundown house on the site; but if the place had ever existed as described in 1953, it certainly had changed in the interim. I tried to trace the ownership of the property, but at some point it'd been divided and sold off piecemeal. The legal owner in 1954 had been a holding company, which in turn had belonged to another holding company, and so on *ad infinitum*. It was certainly beyond my limited ability to decipher.

There was no record in New York or California that The Phantom Detective Agency had ever existed under that name.

So what was this card doing here? Who could have sent it?

The Phantom Detective, if he'd even existed, had to be long dead. We're talking about a man who would have been born about the year 1900 at the latest—remember, he'd served in World War I.

As I sat there in my old, overstuffed office chair gazing out the window on the quad, watching the coed ants scurrying to their classes, something suddenly occurred to me. Could it be that simple?

I pulled out the local yellow pages, and flipped through the book until I came to the category marked, "Investigators & Investigation Svces." Listed in alphabetical order was an agency called "PDA, Ltd.," with an address on Fifth Street in Redlands, California.

I drove there later that afternoon, and parked across the street from Armando's Mexican Restaurant (they served great seafood soup!). I had to walk up to a second-story office. I opened the plain wood door and entered the room. There was a desk facing me, and behind it sat three individuals. The one in the middle was a slim, silver-haired lady of perhaps seventy-five or eighty.

She stared at me with her intense green eyes, and then she smiled.

"Ah, my dear Professor Simmons," she said. "We've been expecting you."

AUTHOR'S NOTE

When presented with the challenge of recreating The Phantom Detective, I had several options available to me. I could try to mimic the original pulp novels, or advance the character further along in his life, or attempt putting some flesh, so to speak, on the bones of a rather hastily sketched character, or some combination thereof.

I decided that the Phantom's original career had ended with the cessation of the magazine after its twenty-year run in 1953. By then he would have likely been in his early fifties. His original contacts and support group, such as it was, would have faded away one by one. He would have been older, more reflective, and less prone to action.

The world of the 1950s was very different from that of the 1930s, when *The Phantom Detective* was first published. If I was going to pick up the trail of Van Loan's life after his initial retirement, many things would necessarily have to change, even if this ultimately displeased the fans of the original series.

I decided to make a virtue of necessity and to reinvent the Phantom at a new time of his life, with new challenges and new compatriots; and, simultaneously, to make him more human than he'd been portrayed in the original stories.

In the pulps Richard Curtis Van Loan is a veritable killing machine, driven by purpose and anger and bile to eliminate the criminal elements in society. Of course, he's never really successful at this, because all of those over-the-top villains keep coming back in new forms with each successive issue—and he has to wipe them out all over again.

Van Loan eschews sex and social relationships because they might distract him from his purpose, and that purpose has the aura of fanaticism about it. We really know nothing about the person himself, or about his true connections with his family or friends, such as they are.

I wanted to change all that. I felt that there was more to the man than had ever been depicted in the original novels. I had one main question: how would a life that had been devoted to killing hundreds, even thousands of individuals ultimately affect one's nature? It was obvious to me that a man as intelligent as Van Loan could not avoid the issue eventually. Sooner or later his conscience would force his will into a ritual of self-examination, and come up wanting. The collateral damage from all that killing, the suffering that he had inadvertently caused the relatives and associates and friends of the criminals, would inevitably plague a man of conscience with an enormous burden of guilt.

That, it seemed to me, was the key to the character of Richard Van Loan. Because, dear readers, if he *didn't* have a conscience, how could he claim to be any better than the men he was pursuing? The ultimate result of *that* kind of reflection is self-destruction. Whatever else Van Loan might have been or might be in the future, he was, I think, a survivor, and he wouldn't have gone down that path.

So I tried to reconstitute the man using these broad parameters, and to give him a reason to continue fighting the negative elements in society. *This* Phantom will never be as certain about his own motives as the original version was. He will never act as mindlessly as his former self. He will never fail to see the multiple consequences of his actions. And he will never be as merciless as he once was.

For one thing, his compatriots will hold him to a different, higher standard of action. Life was simpler for Richard when he could just pull a trigger and make himself judge, jury, and executioner. The new decade of the fifties doesn't allow him that luxury. This is the era of the Korean and Cold Wars, the threat of nuclear holocaust, and the McCarthy hearings. The world has changed. It's no longer as simple as it was.

The threats are still out there, but he needs assistance to confront them. He requires the information that will be provided by a network of associates: hence the Phantom Detective Agency, or PDA, Ltd.

I hope you enjoy this little excursion into literary fantasy and mystery. I had a great deal of fun researching both the era and the area, as well as recreating the characters themselves. Where necessary to advance the plot, I've occasionally taken a few liberties with the geography and the historical reality of the time. For example, although San Bernardino was well known in Southern California as a wild, wide-open town during the 1930s and '40s, filled with houses of ill repute and hidden gambling casinos, by the time of this novel they'd already been swept away by the local authorities. I've assumed for the sake of the plot that some residue of these activities yet remained in 1953.

Thanks to John Betancourt for rolling the dice. My dearest Mary deserves as usual the utmost credit for being my first reader and my primary sounding-board and my only editor. A tip of the topper too to (or tutu) His High and Mighty Excellency, the Emperor of the Inland Empire, who gave me his *imprimatur* and *nihil obstat* before even seeing the final result. Such wisdom, such self-evident perspicacity will undoubtedly someday be rewarded—but probably not by me!

And I already have an idea for a sequel, *The Nasty Gnomes*!

—Robert Reginald
31 January 2006

ABOUT THE AUTHOR

ROBERT REGINALD is the author of 112 published books and 13,000 short pieces. His recent books include the Nova Europa fantasies, *The Dark-Haired Man; or, The Hieromonk's Tale: A Romance of Nova Europa* (2004), *The Exiled Prince; or, The Archquisitor's Tale: A Romance of Nova Europa* (2004), and *Quæstiones; or, The Protopresbyter's Tale: A Romance of Nova Europa* (2005); two fictional guides to the Deryni universe, *Codex Derynianus* and *Codex Derynianus II* (with Katherine Kurtz, 1998 & 2005); the story collection, *Katydid & Other Critters: Tales of Fantasy and Mystery* (2001); the science fiction trilogy, *War of the Worlds I: Invasion!* (2006), *War of the Worlds II: Operation Crimson Storm* (2006), and *War of the Worlds III: The Martians Strike Back!* (2006); the historical mystery, *The Phantom's Phantom: A Novel of the Phantom Detective Agency: As Taken from the Case Files of Richard Curtis Van Loan, The Phantom* (2006); and the nonfiction works, *Murder in Retrospect: A Selective Guide to Historical Mystery Fiction* (with Jill H. Vassilakos, 2005), *San Quentin: The Evolution of a California State Prison* (with Bonnie L. Petry, 2005), *Classics of Fantastic Literature; or, Les Épines Noires: Selected Review Essays* (with Douglas Menville, 2005), *The Eastern Orthodox Churches: Concise Histories with Chronological Checklists of Their Primates* (2005), *Xenograffiti: Essays on Fantastic Literature and Other Divers Topics* (1996 & 2005), *¡Viva California! Seven Accounts of Life in Early California* (with Mary Wickizer Burgess, 2006), *California Ranchos: Patented Private Land Grants by County* (with Burgess McK. Shumway & Mary Wickizer Burgess, 2006), *Across the Wide Missouri: A Diary of a Journey from Virginia to Missouri in 1819 and Back Again in 1822, with a Description of the City of Cincinnati* (with Mary Wickizer Burgess, 2006), *BP 300: An Annotated Bibliography of the Publications of the Borgo Press, 1976-1998* (with Mary Wickizer Burgess, 2006), *Cal State Cooks, 1965-2005: Selected Recipes from the Administration, Faculty, and Staff of California State University, San Bernardino, on the Fortieth Anniversary of the Founding of the Campus* (with Johnnie Ann Ralph, 2006), *CSUSB Faculty Authors, Composers, and Playwrights: A Bibliography of Forty Years of Publishing Monographs and Recordings, 1965-2005* (1996 & 2006); and *Trilobite Dreams; or, The Autodidact's Tale: A Romance of Autobiography* (2006).

Made in the USA